[signature: Keith Palmer]

Of Una, Crime,
And A Boy Who Slipped Through Time

By
Keith Palmer

Also by Keith Palmer

We, The Outcasts of a Killing Sun

The Mystery of the Wailing Ghost Child

For
my family, near and far -
a global community

Chapter 1

It was early spring and the first flowers were beginning to emerge from their winter sleep. Una sat on her satchel by the stone marker and thought about the day ahead. It was Saturday so she had no need to rush away for school. She felt at peace with the world already.

Today she wore a white blouse and long black skirt, she smoothed the soft material to where it met her ankles, slightly above the line of her shiny leather shoes. She wore this same colour outfit every day. Her signature.

Weak sunlight filtered through the trees and the air still held a chill, so she had thrown a light jacket over her shoulders as she left home.

Now she brushed her black hair into place and examined her black varnished nails closely. Moonlight Zombie. A new one she'd found at the chemist that week, and she was pleased with the sharp contrast it gave against her pale skin.

'Still obsessed with the nails, I see!' The boy had appeared from nowhere and propped himself on the low stone marker.

'Edward! Good to see you here.' Una greeted him. It had been her hope to catch him there by his own grave.

'Where else would I be?' The boy quipped.

'Exactly so.' The girl said and she eyed him up and down. As always he looked a mess. A threadbare work shirt and oily dungarees, a handkerchief knotted about his neck and a pair of distressed boots tied about with string to his ankles.

Una noted the grubby hands, his unwashed face and his matted and uncombed hair. But at least he looked better fed this time.

'Who's caring for you these days, Edward?' She asked. 'You look a mess.'

'I'm a working boy now, Una. I care for myself. I don't need anyone to dress me for school, and I don't have time for unnecessary vanities such as personal hygiene. Not in my line of work anyway.' He bent a leg to polish his boot using the arm of his shirt sleeve.

'You still need to take care of yourself, Edward, and school is so important.' Una admonished him.

'Not in my line of work it isn't. All I need to know is how to lead the horse forward at a safe pace, ensure the safety of the tram, help the passengers on and off. And to clear up dung from the road, of course. No qualifications necessary.'

Una screwed her nose. 'Do you enjoy that?' She asked.

'It's my life.' He replied. 'I spend my days in good company. I potter with the tram workings and I care for the horses. At the end of the day I get paid enough to keep me and my mam with a roof.' He thought a moment then added. 'It's more fun than going to school.'

'But don't you miss children of your own age and the teachers and learning about the world and its amazing places?' Una asked. ' I just can't imagine life without my friends or school routines.'

'I miss Sebastien and his minibeasts, and aunt Aggie with her stories, but I have my own family now, and my own time and my own place in history.'

Una nodded. 'You do indeed Edward, and that's a fine thing.'

She recalled now how lonely Edward had been when she had first met him a year ago. Then they were both at the same school and so very different nobody would believe they could ever be close friends. Then the accident happened which ended Edward's life.

'At least I can't smell those musty clothes now that you're a ghost.' Una said. Edward thumped her playfully between the shoulder blades.

A grating sound echoed from the church to interrupt their chatter before Edward's thump on the shoulder could escalate into all out war.

The great wooden door swung slowly open revealing the cool church interior and a cloaked figure who emerged from the shadows stepping with purpose towards the pair. Edward immediately leapt into the air and shouted. 'It's the vicar, scram!' And without waiting for Una raced away down the path towards the row of lofty horse chestnut trees. Una hurriedly collected her satchel and was about to flee too when she remembered that the vicar was always kindly and polite, and that Edward's fear of him was wholly unwarranted. So she halted her flight and turned instead to greet the man.

'Ah, Una, isn't it?' The vicar said as he drew closer. 'We met in the autumn when you used our programme of food aid packages. Do you remember?' Una nodded yes. 'You were so kind then that I wondered if you might help with another community issue we've had thrown our way just now?' He awaited an answer with his bony fingers plaited in a cradle.

Before she had chance to reply Edward returned, puffing and panting. He doubled over at a safe distance. 'Why didn't you leg it, Una?' He asked between gulps for air. 'Because I don't need to, the vicar is my friend.' She replied softly.

The vicar turned his neck to see who the girl was talking to but no-one was there.

'Pardon?' He asked.

'He can't see me because I'm a ghost.' Edward informed Una.

'Yes, I'm aware of that.' She replied. 'Nobody can see you apart from me, for some inexplicable reason.'

'It's a punishment!' Edward said and laughed at his own joke.

Una returned her attention to the vicar saying, 'I'm happy to help in any way I can.'

'You are so kind, Una. Can you follow me into the church and I'll introduce you to our 'little' problem?' The vicar emphasised the word 'little' leaving Una to wonder at his meaning while he strode off with giant strides towards the church.

'Well, actually it's not so little, as you'll see.' He called back to Una who had chased after him.

'Watch out, Una it might be a trap!' Edward warned pulling at her sleeve.

'Of course it's not a trap. Whoever heard of vicars setting traps. Sometimes you say such nonsense, Edward.'

The vicar turned in mid stride and checked the empty space Una seemed to be speaking into.

'Ah, I see, you have one of those invisible friends!' He exclaimed.

'I certainly do,' Una replied, 'although I would hardly call him a friend.' She gave Edward a cool stare.

Edward folded his arms and grinned mischievously. 'Well good luck to you!' He said and being unwilling to follow her into the church ghosted back to his own grave stone.

It was cooler inside and Una's nostrils filled with that familiar musky dampness which she always associated with churches and other old buildings.

'Now, Una, in my role as a member of the local community I have had a challenge set me and knowing what a caring individual you have proved yourself in the past I wonder if you might be able to offer some assistance.'

This lamppost of a man flexed his bony white knuckles and his bushy grey eyebrows bent low to meet hers.

'I can certainly try.' Una replied hesitantly, beginning to feel like the fly that has been lured into a spider's web, while on the other hand feeling impatient to discover what this mysterious challenge might be.

'Excellent!' The vicar replied and straightened suddenly to stand towering above her. 'Follow into my office and I'll introduce you to the 'little' problem.'

Una was familiar enough with the stuffy little office with its rows of hymn books and racks of damp clothing, she had spent an hour or two there searching through records of births and deaths when she had her own little mystery to solve, the mystery of an unmarked gravestone which she had discovered in the church grounds.

At first glance the office seemed no different to her last visit, but then she gasped in a mixture of surprise and delight when she caught sight of the challenge which the vicar needed help with.

It was a large slumbering dog, curled up contentedly on a rug spread across the centre of the floor.

'Allow me to introduce you to Nelson.' The vicar said and at the sound of his name, the dog's ears pricked sharply upright and he immediately became alert, lifting a huge brown head until two twinkling black eyes gazed expectantly back into Una's.

She dropped her satchel to the floor and approached the dog, cautiously at first, longing to stroke the animal's fine hair but also apprehensive of the power of the creature.

'You don't have to worry, Una, I have it on the very best of authority that Nelson is perfectly safe with young people. He's a Doberman and they have a reputation for being calm and loyal.'

Una plucked out a hand as a token of friendship and the head nosed forward in return sniffing at her fingers.

'Hello, Nelson.' She coaxed and the dog responded by giving her a friendly lick on the hand and a warm nuzzle with its nose.

'Sadly, Nelson is lost and his owner unknown, so he is both homeless and ownerless, hence our community church must take responsibility for his well-being until other arrangements can be made. Or his rightful owner found. You see, the church caters for more than just the needs of humans!'

Una continued to make friends with the dog, but then frowned suddenly. 'I'm sure my parents wouldn't allow me to own a dog, they have their plates full enough as it is looking after me!'

'Yes, I'm sure they have. Not!' The vicar laughed. 'I don't expect you to adopt him, Una, I just need a trustworthy dog walker, someone to take him off our hands for an hour or two now and then. There's so much work to be done in the church and what with the craft fair next weekend and Easter looming, we do need a bit of a break from dog sitting from time to time.'

Una's face brightened. 'Oh, I'd love to take him for a walk. We could explore the town, or I can take him to meet my friends and we can get to know each other better.'

The vicar soon found a lead in Nelson's makeshift bed and passed it to Una. 'You can start work immediately, if you'd like to!' He suggested.

Una attached the wide leather strap to the collar around the dog's neck. She noticed it had a number of large silver studs and the name, 'Nelson' engraved into a rectangular shield. Nelson responded by leaping up and down in excitement and anticipation.

'I'm afraid he's still quite young and boisterous, but he will settle down after a minute of two.' The vicar assured her.

Una gave a pat to Nelson's shoulder rubbing her hand against the short wiry hair, feeling the warmth and firm ripple of muscle beneath.

'What say you and I set off immediately for a test drive, Nelson?' She asked and the eager dog pulled on the lead as a mark of approval. Off they went, striding out through the tall church doors.

'Take care!' The vicar called after her, but too late, the pair were already out of hearing and weaving between the rows of horse chestnut trees on the opposite side of the path. Leaving the quiet of the church behind, Una steered a route down the main street passing a small queue of passengers waiting patiently in line for the next bus. They shuffled warily to one side allowing Nelson a wide berth. Then a group of shoppers edged aside too.

I do like this, Una thought to herself, smiling inside. Normally people stubbornly held their ground, or being a young girl she would be expected to give way, sometimes having to step into the path of oncoming traffic before skipping back onto the pavement when space allowed. Nor could she fail to notice how perfectly the smart black body, proud face and finely groomed hair of the dog perfectly matched her own neat appearance as their six legs stepped in harmony along the street.

She had to give herself a quick vanity check. The last thing Una wanted was to adorn herself with a live fashion accessory! She knew better than do that. Sebastien would be horrified. Even so, she already felt a certain accord, like the carefully arranged notes of a tune, with her new canine friend.

From time to time Nelson craned his neck back to catch her eye as if to assure himself they were taking the correct route, and each time Una responded with a positive. 'Go for it Nelson, you're a star!'

They passed opposite the little secondhand bookshop where Una caught sight of the owner, Vincent berthed in a window seat.

By chance he happened to look up at exactly the same moment and Una watched with delight to see him jump in surprise and then stand, open mouthed like a statue.

She smiled and waved a hand but the bookshop owner was too shocked to return her greeting.

Now Una guided her companion away from the main street and the noise of the traffic to explore less well trodden avenues lined with budding lime trees. Their conversation continued under the green shade with the intelligent dog listening in keenly to her voice and seeming to catch her meaning.

'Go left here. Turn right. Walk straight on.' She instructed and the clever Doberman soon latched on to the different tones and obeyed each command.

That is until they came eventually to one particular junction where the houses had thinned and the neatly tended gardens spread out wide and expansive.

'Straight on, Nelson!' Una ordered, but this time her companion misunderstood it seemed and veered left. Una gave a gentle tug on the lead to correct the error, repeating in a firmer voice, 'No Nelson, go straight!'

But Nelson only tugged more insistently to the left.

In the end Una decided it was easier to follow Nelson's wishes and follow left.

'I'm sorry to call rank on you, Nelson, but I should remind you that I'm the one pulling the strings here, or at least I think that's the way of it!'

Nelson halted at the next crossroad then led on when the road was clear of traffic. 'I don't even know where we are anymore!' Una complained and they made yet another turn. Nelson craned his face towards hers and his eyes seemed to twinkle with mischief.

'Where are you taking me, Nelson?' She asked in her one sided conversation.

The answer soon became clear when Nelson drew up at an old wooden gate, set in a tall brick wall which surrounded a private garden. He lay down in the pavement and waited expectantly, but expectantly for what Una couldn't say.

She gave a tickle to his ear and jiggled the lead to tell him she wanted to move on, but Nelson whined and seemed determined to stay put right there in the middle of the pavement with his head rested between two paws and his big black eyes pleading with hers.

Eventually this strange behaviour aroused in Una's mind a suspicion about the ownership of the property where Nelson had parked himself.

'Could this be your master's home?' She asked and the smart dog gave a soft whimper.

Una wanted to investigate further, but the ancient wall was high, much too tall for her to peer over, and the gate was enclosed completely within the brickwork.

She tested the latch which immediately caused Nelson to spring up in anticipation. He began pawing at the wood and sniffed the frame, expecting the gate to be opened. But it was locked firmly closed.

'I'm afraid we are locked out!' Una declared. Nelson gave another whine then returned to his resting place on the pavement.

Una was frustrated for it seemed to her there was no way of taking a peek inside, which is what she had a mind to do. So she looked up and down the street, and there not too far away she observed one of those service boxes, of the type used to house telephone lines or similar cables. The green box was set neatly up against the wall.

The opportunity the box presented was too enticing to miss so Una made her way to the box and prised an experimental toe in-between a course of the crumbly mortar work in the wall then hoisted herself awkwardly upwards until at length she sat astride the top of the green box.

Now she was able to grip a hand to the wall's cap some eight feet above the pavement, which she soon did, and once she had lifted her head above was rewarded with a splendid view across wooded grounds and beyond to an overgrown garden.

'It's a secret garden, just like the one in the story!' She called down to Nelson who was waiting patiently by the base.

But what a scene of neglect it was!

A number of mature trees were set in a broad circle following the perimeter wall, their sweeping branches intertwined such that only a weak sunlight penetrated to the ground beneath. Beyond these lay a tangle of shrubs and bushes which spread like weeds.

Then with a gasp of surprise Una made out the shape of an old house, hidden almost entirely by the screen of bushes.

It looked from a distance to be built in the style of a medieval castle for the roof had a pair of upturned witches hats built into the eaves, each one with its own tiny window. Filling the upper storey were four gothic windows, tall, black and mysterious. Then at ground level and boarded over with wooden shuttering, was a further set of gothic windows and a heavy wooden door set slap bang in the middle.

Una sensed it had once made a fine family home, but now it seemed derelict. And in all probability, crawling with ghosts!

She immediately made a mental note to report back the finding to her ghost hunting friends, Sebastien and Verity, they were always keen to discover new hauntings or mysterious houses to investigate.

As she pictured their reaction to her news in her mind, she heard the thump of a revving engine approaching fast and then passing by on the road. Next moment a white van pulled up beyond the gate at a set of double doors further along the street. There followed the scrape of doors being drawn apart. Someone was entering the grounds through a vehicle access further along.

Una bent her head down behind the wall and peeked through a gap to watch as several hefty men jumped from the van and pinned the gates open.

One of them gave a furtive glance up and down the street then rapped on the side to wave the van inside. The men quickly clanked the gates closed behind them and jogged behind the van to join the driver and a front seat passenger outside the house door.

'Perhaps they're moving furniture in, or out.' Thought Una. She continued to watch as the driver and an elegantly dressed woman passenger joined the others in the porch to the front door. Una counted six in all. They looked nothing like you might expect for a typical family moving into a new home. They had no common features.

One of them turned in Una's direction and appeared to look directly into her eyes. She shrank further back, but not before catching the striking features of a long miserable moon shaped face sprinkled with grey stubble and a black patch covering one eye.

'A pirate!' Una whispered to herself.

He took an object from his jacket pocket, ran it into the lock then slid the door open. The next moment all six had melted into the shadowy interior of the house.

'How odd!' Una exclaimed under her breath.

She lowered herself back to the pavement where Nelson waited patiently.

'Something very strange is going on in there, Nelson.' She declared.'I can sense it. And I wouldn't want to meet any of those characters down a dark alley at night, that's for certain.'

Crime did not feature strongly in Una's life, she came from a well to do family with well to do friends and well to do neighbours. That people might have unlawful intentions was quite novel to her and intrigued her.

'We should return this way next time and find a way to unlock the gate. I'd love to know what mischief they're up to.'

Nelson made no comment but a creasing of his brows inward like an inverted seagull's wing made her think that he too had his suspicions about them.

He growled his approval and sensing he was not to pass through the gate on this occasion stood ready to depart. 'Time for us to return you to the church.' Una said. 'It's been fun getting to know you Nelson, but my parents will be fretting about where I am!' Nelson gave Una's knee a reassuring nuzzle to say he understood, then set off at a brisk pace back towards the church pulling the girl along behind.

Chapter 2

Sebastien dragged a net between the stems of stiff irises and a clump of water-mint while balancing on the slippery bank. After a second sweep he lifted the sagging handle from the dripping water and drew out the net onto the wooden boards. His wrist gave a twist and he emptied the contents to form a muddy heap on the deck.

Peering in closely, his fingers drew back the knotty clots while he patiently unravelled the parts and laid each sorted clump into a neat line.

Suddenly he let out a, 'got you,' and cradled a glistening black creature in the palm of his hand. He plopped the thrashing dragon into a bucket by his ankle. After a moment or two he had filtered a second from the weed and added the nymph to his collection. Then he scaled back up the wooden boarded bank using one arm for balance and gripping the bucket handle with the other.

'Tales of the Riverbank?' A voice asked, and there was Verity hovering over him like a crime scene investigator. 'I see you have detained a couple of suspects in the cell.' She added peering into the bucket.

Sebastien took hold of the girl's arm offered and lifted himself up.

'Just take a look at these beauties.' He said shifting the bucket closer to her face.

'What are they?' Verity asked. She took a magnifier from her pocket and raised the glass to an eye. The little creatures were made large under the magnifier and given the appearance of mythical monsters.

'They're dragonfly nymphs.' Sebastien answered. 'Fierce predators. They live in the pond through the winter before climbing up a reed stem in the spring and turning into a fully grown dragonfly under the warming sunshine. Would you like to hold one?'

'No thanks!' Verity replied curtly eyeing the powerful jaws and the pronged tail which danced against the air once removed from the familiar pull of water.

'Shouldn't you put them back, they won't be able to breathe?' She said. The boy lowered the creature gently back into the bucket and in an instant it merged like a shadow into the murky water at the base.

'To think that in a short time these drab water living creatures will turn into beautiful winged masters of the skies.'

'It's truly fascinating.' Verity said, admiring Sebastien's enthusiasm for the natural world though she had no great love for it herself.

'I'm here for the meeting.' She said to change the subject.

'Right. I'd forgotten about the meeting. Too busy playing with dragons. We'd better get organised, you know how Una likes everything to be spot on time!'

They crossed to the base of the oak tree. It was by far the oldest living thing in the nature zone, and quite possibly older than the Victorian school itself.

A cord dangled below the lowest branch and Sebastien gave it a tug to release a ladder which uncoiled noisily to the ground.

'I much preferred our lovely old tram.' Verity complained as she climbed the ladder. 'It was so much easier to get into.' When she reached the top rung she opened a door into a wooden treehouse and crawled inside.

While this happened Una arrived and joined Sebastien at the base.

She was still abuzz with thoughts of the strange goings-on at the old house and couldn't wait to tell her friends about it, to see their reactions. Of course she was dying to tell them about Nelson too, but a dog story could never match the exciting prospect of a ghost hunt, or even a crime investigation.

Una negotiated the ladder awkwardly in her long skirt taking care not to damage her nails or scratch her leather shoes in the process. Appearances, she told herself, must be maintained to immaculate standards, even under adverse conditions.

Sebastien by contrast hoisted himself up the bucking steps in pirate fashion, with much poise and balance. He needed to impress the team. It was after all his idea to build a tree house in the school's nature zone, and the tree house was where he spent much of his free time, so he must at least give the impression of being at home there.

It was at the beginning of the year that his project began. He had discovered a stash of unwanted wooden boards hidden away in one of the school's storerooms. He asked Aggie, the old caretaker if he might take a few to create a slipway down the slippery banks to the pond. Aggie was all for the idea and even lent Sebastien the tools he would need.

'But don't tell the headmaster.' She warned. 'You know what an old skinflint Mr Pinchcod is! He'll want to know exactly how many planks you've had, how many nails you've used and who's going to pay for it all!'

Once he'd finished nailing the planks together to form the slipway and finding there were many left over, Sebastien had the brainwave of constructing the tree house.

Firstly he nailed a wooden base into a hollow of the old oak tree made by a tripod of three branches. Next he added three sides and a low flat roof. After that he found an old glass cloche frame which he used to make a forth side and this allowed sunlight to filter through into the space. It was almost perfect.

Una contributed cushions and a pair of yellow curtains borrowed from her own home and Verity pinned up a wallpaper of news articles to the walls. Suddenly the compact little space was turned into a cosy meeting place just right for their committee meetings.

'Number one on today's agenda is to agree a name for our meeting room.' Verity began, reading from her tablet once they were settled.

'I love naming things.' Una exclaimed. It was true, she'd been fascinated almost from birth about names and their meanings. It all began with her own name, Una, meaning unique, special, one of a kind, all of which she honestly felt described her own qualities perfectly.

'How about Nature's Retreat?' Sebastien suggested.

Una frowned. 'Sebastien! We're a group of ghost hunters, but all you ever think about is nature!' Sebastien looked glum.

Several more names were suggested but they were either too vague or too off topic, then Verity suggested, 'The Eyrie.' She paused to let the others get a feel for the word then added, 'It's the name given to an eagle's nest, but it also sounds almost identical to the word 'eerie' meaning a strange or unexpected event.' Sebastien shot her a look of approval.

'I see, like in a ghostly sense.' Una said.

'I like it.' Sebastien enthused. 'Eyrie is like a homophone weaving together the meanings of an eagle's nest and that of a strange occurrence.'

So it was decided without any further debate.

'Next on the agenda is the question of Aggie and whether we ought to invite her to be a member of the group.'

'I'd love to invite her, but I doubt she could climb the ladder.' Una observed, and the other two nodded their agreement.

'I don't think the rope would take her weight.' Sebastien added rather unkindly.

'You're right, Sebastien. We'll put off making a decision for now.' Verity said, and she moved to the final item on her list.

'Una says she has discovered a haunted house for us to investigate.'

At the mention of haunted house Sebastien suddenly sat bolt upright.

'Haunted house? What haunted house? You didn't tell me about a haunted house, Una!' He shouted.

'I haven't had time, Sebastien. I only discovered it yesterday and I'm not exactly sure it is haunted.' Una admitted, slightly embarrassed by jumping to such a conclusion. 'But I am sure something weird is going on in there.'

'A haunted house in the area will make a brilliant subject for the school magazine, Verity. All the kids will want to visit it!' Sebastien continued. 'We could charge an entry fee. How did you come to find it, Una?'

'I was doing my new job, dog walking Nelson for the vicar when we came across this house surrounded by a tall wall. Nelson wanted to go inside so I climbed the wall to take a peek inside, and there it was, as haunted a house as ever I saw one!'

'Describe to us what it's like!' Sebastien demanded.

'Tall windows, black and mysterious, unkept gardens and everything hidden inside a high brick wall like someone wanted to keep it a secret. All very spooky.'

'Sounds perfect for supernatural going-ons.' Verity agreed.

'But even more disturbing.' Una continued. 'Just as I peeked inside, a white van pulled up onto the drive. It was filled with the shadiest looking characters you ever could imagine. They scoured the grounds furtively to make sure they weren't being watched then promptly let themselves in through the front door like they owned the place.'

'Really?' Verity exclaimed.

'Except they obviously didn't because the meanest one turned to look right into my eyeballs as he snitched open the door and I can tell you he was up to no good. As certain a master criminal as ever I saw one.'

'Let's investigate, Una. It sounds amazing!' Sebastien exclaimed. 'We can check it out this weekend.'

'Let's make it Friday after school.' Verity suggested. 'Then we'll have the whole weekend to work on it. Una can bring Nelson along for us to meet if she wants to and he'll give us an alibi for being there if anyone asks any awkward questions!'

So the date was settled and soon after Una made her excuses and scaled down the ladder to make her way to the churchyard. She wanted to catch up with Edward.

She found him crouched in the long grass by his own stone marker and threw down her satchel to sit on breathing in the fresh spring air after her brisk walk.

'I can't be seen, felt or heard by anyone but you, Una. How is that possible?' Edward asked while she recovered her breath.

Una deliberated over the question a moment or two then replied.

'We were both in the stockroom on that day it caught fire, on the day you perished in the smoke. Maybe something happened then, something to create a bond of some sort between us, girl and ghost.'

'Yes, I do remember. It was the day I became transported back to my own true time, to continue my life in the century before yours began.' He examined his grubby clothing.

'Now I work on the town's trams, I care for the tram horses and I put them to bed at night, just as any working Victorian boy might do.'

He climbed down from the stone marker to join Una sitting on the grass.

'But every now and then there's a force which draws me forwards to this time, forward to where you are, to this particular place.'

'I think you've become unstable Edward. As a result of your accident.' Una observed.

Do you mean mentally unstable? Like as I'm simply imagining the whole time travel thing?' Edward asked.

'No Edward. I'm thinking more of being physically unstable.' Una replied. 'Like the creatures Sebastien keeps in his pond'

'Frogspawn?' Sebastien exclaimed in surprise.

'Yes exactly so! Millions and millions of tadpoles emerging from spawn, turn into frogs and then perishing. Every one of them is identical to the next one and there's never any variation.'

'But I am different!' Edward declared.

'Yes that's just it! You're right! Every once in a zillion times, nature produces a tadpole that mutates, that acts or looks differently to all the others. I think that one is you, Edward!'

Edward returned to balance on his stone marker and pulled his knees up thoughtfully beneath his chin. He sat there like an elf on a toadstool.

Edward knew that Una was still upset about him being so different, which was odd for a person whose aim in life was to be unique, someone who valued individuality above everything else. But Una wanted him to be normal, just like everyone else so that he might fit in.

'You don't need to worry for me, Una, I'm fine about being invisible. Usually the only company I have are the tram horses and they never have anything interesting to say anyway. So being here with you is like a gift of sorts.'

Una gave a brief smile. 'I'd prefer to have you with me full time, as a real friend, rather than a part time ghost friend!'

'I know. It's a strange situation for you.' Edward agreed. 'But consider my situation, caught between two different times each a hundred years apart. One moment I'm leading a horses up and down the tramlines and the next I'm being dragged away to a different time, to haunt you in this increasingly unfamiliar future world.'

'I'm not complaining, Edward. I love having you as a friend, and I wouldn't change a thing if it meant never seeing you again.'

Edward shrugged his shoulders sadly. 'I'm the boy who became split between two worlds, a mutation, as you rightly say.'

Una jumped up to gave her friend a hug. 'I'm sorry, Edward. I'm such a selfish person, always thinking of myself. It must be extremely confusing for you too.'

Their conversation was interrupted suddenly by the sound of footsteps approaching and the vicar came striding from the church with Nelson bounding along beside him.

'Ah, Una good to see you.' The vicar said by way of greeting while Nelson wasted no time on words but promptly snuggled his wet nose against Una's outstretched knuckles. She flicked his ear playfully.

'I wonder if you might have a little time to walk Nelson?' The vicar asked.

'I'd love to.' Una replied and she took the lead.

But unusually, Nelson pulled away and growled fiercely showing a set of sharp white teeth. Edward quickly backed away and hid behind a tree.

The vicar was taken aback. 'How very odd. I've never seen Nelson be aggressive like that before.' He said.

'It's alright, Nelson.' Una cooed in a reassuring voice and the dog settled down. 'I think he's been spooked by a bird, or something in the tree.'

The vicar peered into the tree's branches but saw nothing unusual. Then he asked, 'I wonder Una, are you practicing for a part in a drama?' Una raised her brows and the vicar added, 'As I approached you seemed to be speaking out aloud to yourself.'

Now Una understood. 'I guess I am practicing for a drama in a sense.' She replied. 'Life itself can be a bit of a drama at times.'

She patted Nelson on his flank and turned to speak to Edward. 'Want to come for a walk with us, invisible ghost boy?' She asked.

She set out down the path without awaiting his reply and the vicar shook his head as he watched her depart, chattering away as it seemed to herself.

Chapter 3

Una stopped by the secondhand bookshop after her walk
with Nelson. A pang of guilt tugged at her conscience
because she hadn't bought a single book from Vincent in the
last month and she knew how much he relied on her trade.
But with one thing and another she'd been too busy for
reading.

She threw her satchel to the floor and slumped back lazily
into a worn-out armchair in the snug room.

As usual Bookworm leaped down from a shelf as soon as
she spotted the inviting lap, but on this particular day the
lazy cat hesitated and approached nervously sniffing at the
pleat of her skirt.

'Ah, it's the scent of Nelson lingering there that makes you
wary! But fear not, Bookworm, I haven't brought the beast
with me!' The old cat continued to sniff suspiciously
anyway, no doubt building a picture of the creature from the
scent clues until finally the dog profile was complete, then
satisfied there was no danger the old cat stretched out her
claws and sprang into Una's lap.

A pink tongue licked away any remaining dog scents from
her delicate white fingers before the cat settled down
contentedly. 'All is forgiven, you may now enjoy my purrs.'
She seemed to say.

Una scratched around inside her satchel and found a small
metal object. It was the toy soldier Edward had given her, a
gift for helping him rescue his toy box from the fire. Its
surface was dark and scratched like old gunmetal, but the
lead toy felt warm and smooth to her fingers.

Una had heard it said that such Victorian toys carried health risks. Exposure to the lead could damage the brain and result in a coma, or even death in extreme cases. Even so, she found the toy fascinating and she willingly flirted with death, as might superman in the presence of the deadly kryptonite.

Yet it wasn't the danger that intrigued Una, but the knowledge that the toy had come to her as a present from the distant past, had skipped a hundred years or more to be in her possession. A gift from a ghost.

'Ah, there you are my number one customer. I thought you had abandoned me and sailed away to lands anew.' The belly came navigating between isles of books and laid a cup of hot tea on the broad arm of her chair, carefully so as not to spill a drop of the precious brown liquid.

'Hi, Vincent. No of course I haven't abandoned you, it's just that I've been rather busy recently.'

'Yes, we had noticed hadn't we Bookworm? We watched you passing from the crow's nest. I must say you did cut an elegant figurehead striding along with your new friend.' Vincent said with an edge of jealousy to his voice.

'He's called Nelson and he's a Doberman.' Una explained taking a sip of the tea. 'Just now he's lost and ownerless so I have to take him for a daily exercise until a new home can be found for him.'

'Ah, I see. Well yes, you do make quite a statement the two of you as you walk the decks together.'

'Thank you, Vincent, but I feel I need some guidance on how to care for him. I rather hoped you might have a book or two on dog care to help me?'

Vincent punched his palms into the folds of his hips and held a posture like a proud naval captain. 'Would I have a book or two? Just give me five chains of a ship's anchor.' He said. The belly sailed over the horizon to return some minutes later gripping a paperback between finger and thumb.

'Am I not the number one best book seller this side of the Greenwich Meridian line?' The shopkeeper asked and laid the book on her lap.

'I knew you'd be in here sooner or later needing my help, so there you have it!'

"The Doberman Pinscher, an Owner's Guide.' Una read from the title. 'Thanks, Vincent, that's perfect!' Una flicked open the cover then just in time remembered she must pay Vincent. She passed him a pair of coins from her satchel.

A ship's bell sounded and shook the dusty air.

'Another customer, Bookworm! Business has never been so good!' The shop owner proclaimed and the lazy cat stirred at the sound of her name but just as quickly recoiled into a sleepy ring when no food appeared.

'This is perfect, Vincent.' Una said thumbing through the pages of the manual.

The bell tinkled again.

'You've struck gold with a Doberman.' Vincent told her, 'Loyal, trustworthy, super intelligent, good with families. But enough about me! Make yourself at home, Una and enjoy your read!'

The bell rang a third time.

'What is the world coming to? I've never had so many customers!' Vincent exclaimed.

Una was about to thank him when heavy footsteps signalled an arrival into the room and a thick set man muscled up close to Vincent and cornered him like a boxer intimidating an opponent.

'Oi, Captain Pugwash, how does a customer get some service in this worm infested hole?' The man asked in a deep growl.

Vincent tried to back off from the aggressive customer.

'I'm dreadfully sorry.' He squeaked. 'Una and I were caught up in a friendly chat. Can I be of assistance?'

'This book. How much is it?' A clammy hand thrust the book into Vincent's face.

Before the bookseller had time to answer a second thug came into the tiny room. This one was thin, like a weasel, with a starved, moon shaped face and one intense, staring eye, the second one being hidden behind a black patch.

'We want books about Ravenscar. History. Settlements. Maps of the area. Anything like that.' The one eyed man demanded abruptly.

Vincent struggled to muster a reply, his mind still wrestling with the Captain Pugwash insult.

'One pound fifty.' He gulped at last.

'Daylight robbery!' The man complained, and now a stylishly dressed woman with fake blond hair breezed in and linked arms with him.

'Give him a quid and call it a deal, Tinker.' She told him. The man took a coin from his pocket and flicked it at the shopkeeper. Vincent fumbled to his knees and crawled over the floorboards to collect it.

'So, do you have anything on Ravenscar or not?' The man with the one eyed stare asked again impatiently.

'Of course I do!' Vincent replied, now thoroughly rattled. 'Local history books are my speciality. Follow me, please.' Vincent led the pair away down the creaking corridor.

All the time this little drama played out, Una was shrunk into the leathery folds of her armchair, holding her breath and hiding her face behind the delicate bone china teacup. For certain, these were the self same gang she had seen drive up to the old house in their white van just a few days earlier.

But the drama was not yet over, for now two new men creaked into the room and began sifting through the shelves of books, completely ignoring Una in her chair.

Eventually one of them pulled a spine from the shelf and after examining the cover a moment passed the book to his friend.

'Hey, Ferrit take a sniff at this.' He said.

'I told you Richter, I'm not interested in books.' Came the reply.

'I know you're not, but this one's all about smugglers of old who operated here on this very coast. That's what we are, Ferrit, modern day smugglers.'

'I still don't want to read about it. I know how to smuggle without reading a book about it.' The one called Ferrit replied. He shoved his hands inside his pockets and looked bored.

'I'll get it anyhow, Tinker might need it for night time reading.'

The bell tinkled again, this time telling of a departure and the two men rushed out of the room to catch up with whoever had just left.

'And don't bother coming back, we can do without your types here!' Vincent called out after the departing customers.

He aimed his complaints at Una, since the offenders had already left, but when he looked to her usual armchair it was bare, the tea in the cup cold and the unfortunate Bookworm abandoned to an empty seat.

Una had raced out just in time to see the white van disappear around a side street.

She sprinted off in the opposite direction lifting her skirt high above her knees. Una knew of a short cut which avoided the irksome one way system that vehicles were compelled to follow.

As she raced by the rows of wide shop windows she caught a flash of her own reflection in the glass, a slim figure with long black hair streaming out behind as she dashed by.

Una had never thought of herself as a detective or for that matter a movie star, but on seeing reflected such an elegant figure in the windows, with trendy white blouse, black dress and shiny boots, the idea was suddenly brought to her mind, or perhaps even the impression of an ace spy hot on the case of master criminals.

She intended to follow the suspects in their van to discover exactly what mischief the no good crooks were up to.

She arrived by the communications box and stood panting against its hard metal casing. But there was no time for rest.

No sooner had she caught her breath than there came a scrape of brakes and the sound of gates being slid open. Una legged up to the lintel of the wall cursing the abrasive brickwork for cutting into her ankles and chaffing her delicate fingernails.

She took a hair-raising leap over the wall into the overgrown garden then ducked quickly behind a large overgrown laurel bush. From this place of leafy concealment she was able to watch the white van rev up the drive before pulling to a halt outside the main entrance.

Doors were thrown open and several men jumped from the cab followed by the glamorous woman and the one they called Tinker. Just as before Una watched that one eagle eye scan the grounds with its intense glower, then they all slipped briskly inside.

Una made up her mind to find an alternative entry from where she might spy on the gang without being herself observed.

Using the jungle-like undergrowth as cover, she slowly edged around the perimeter grounds until she came at last to a point where it was possible to dash across a short strip of lawn and hide below the wall at the rear of the house. But to her dismay there was no easy access to the property, for as at the front of the house, the ground floor windows had been boarded over to prevent eyes from prying inside. Una turned her gaze to the upper storey where, to her relief she found the windows were not boarded, and furthermore, one particularly grand window had its own balcony which might allow her a good view into the interior. If only she could reach it.

And there was the answer, an ancient wisteria whose grisly branches hugged the wall and climbed in steps upwards to a point only a metre from the balcony itself.

The knotty wood made a comfortable climb for Una, much easier than the drainpipe she often used to escape her bedroom at night when her parents believed she was safely tucked up in bed.

Not all went according to plan however, for as she heaved herself upwards, bit by bit, the dry and withered branches threatened to buckle under the unexpected weight. For a heart stopping moment Una feared a nasty fall to the ground when only the nasties inside the house would hear her cries for help.

But at last with her heart thudding Una made a lunge for the balcony platform. For a terrifying moment her legs kicked air before her fingertips made contact with the base. From there she was able to drag herself upwards to rest flat on the hard concrete base and gather breath.

Once she had recovered, She tried to make herself as thin as an after eight mint by holding her breath while edging slowly across to one side of the window. She was tempted to risk a peek inside through the wide pane but at that moment Edward suddenly appeared from nowhere and straddled casually across the topmost rail of the balcony.

'What on earth are you doing, Una?' He asked in a puzzled voice.

'Don't blow my cover, Edward, if those crooks spot me I'll be in for the high jump!'

Edward peered into the dark window. 'There's no one in there.' He said. 'Stupid question, but how can I blow your cover when I'm invisible?'

Una relaxed a little and brushed herself down. 'I'm on a mission, Edward, hot on the trail of a gang of unscrupulous crooks.' She risked a quick glance through the tall window and sure enough the room was empty just as Edward said. 'Not only that, but I'm sure one of the thieves took a book from Vincent's shop without paying for it!' Una had a strong sense of right and wrong and the injustice to her friend seemed to her unforgivable.

'This is such fun, Una! There am I trudging up and down the town with a pair of boring tram horses all day while you're having the most amazing adventure of a lifetime!'

'It's not amazing in the least, Edward. I'd rather be at home helping mum in the kitchen.' Una whispered back. 'And why do you always turn up at the most inconvenient moments?'

'I've no idea, Una. To be honest I was minding my own business, feeding oats to the horses when suddenly, zap! I find myself whisked away through time and perched on the edge of some random balcony. It's seriously irritating.'

'Irritating for you, yes, but what about me? I could be captured at any minute by those ruffians and horribly tortured for eavesdropping on their evil plans!'

Even as Una spoke she saw the shadows of two men enter the room passing directly in front of the window. She quickly ducked down low and watched from a chink in the curtains.

The men's arms were loaded with an assortment of boxes, bags and cases which they dumped carelessly in an untidy pile on a large marble dining table in the centre of the room. Una herself drew back and listened.

The pair were in jovial mood, laughing at their own jokes. They began removing objects from the boxes, inspecting the contents closely and occasionally waving a particularly interesting item for the other to examine.

Una watched their grubby fingers handle watches, gemstones, pearly necklaces, sparkling jewels and other valuable treasures. Each piece was held up to examine in detail, probably to weigh up its value, and then returned to its box or case on the tabletop.

'I knew it! They're up to no good.' Una exclaimed.

As she spoke one of the men crossed close by the window and looked out across the grounds towards a dilapidated building at the farthermost edges of the boundary.

Una ducked back in the nick of time. Her breath caught and her heart jumped into her throat. The very thought of being discovered red handed set her senses reeling in a spin.

'I'm getting out of here while the going's good!' She blurted to Edward.

'I don't blame you.' Edward replied. Even a ghost could appreciate the danger she faced of being discovered there, and while he had no fears for his own safety Edward did worry about his friend, especially as should an emergency arise he could offer little in the way of help.

Una crawled below the window then leapt from the balcony to land heavily against the blue flowered wisteria. Clinging on desperately to the flimsy branches she half fell, half abseiled down the knots of purple foliage as they ripped and snagged at her clothing until finally she parted company with the branches and her feet made solid contact with the ground.

She breathed a sigh of relief.

But as she twisted her hips to escape relief turned to despair. The long barrel of a hunting gun was aimed directly at her tender little nose, hovering just millimetres from that delicate organ. At the opposite end of the barrel, a bent finger hovered over the trigger.

This finger belonged to an unshaven man with hard grey eyes and a thin slit of a mouth. He wore green checked hunting garb, a threadbare shirt which had obviously never been washed in its entire lifetime and a tweed deerstalker hat to contain his grey hair.

Una's heart sank. She should have known the crooks would post a guard on the outside to deter unwanted guests. It was so obvious. Any crook worth his salt would do it, and Una had been caught in the net. She cursed herself for being so young and naive.

'And what may I ask do you think you're up to young madam?' The crook asked in menacing tones.

'This looks serious.' Edward said examining the long muzzle of the hunting gun up close. 'I'd think this thing could blast a hole right through your brains and splatter them out the other side!'

'This is not the time for jokes, Edward.' Una replied, too petrified to invent her usual comical answer. The man's eyes diverted slightly to the space Una had spoke into, but he was far too old and wise to fall for that old trick. 'Answer the question!' He demanded.

'I'm sorry, I only wanted to see what the house looked like inside. My parents are thinking of upgrading.' She said, but the words came out in an unconvincing whisper.

The wiry man shifted his legs and held the gun firmly at shoulder height.

'And how did you gain access to the property?' He asked coldly.

'I'm sorry, but the gate was locked and I know I shouldn't have but I did, I climbed over the wall at the front and jumped in.' Una confessed.

She desperately wanted to give him a good telling off for beginning all his sentences with 'And,' but it didn't feel like this was quite the right moment.

'And so you're up to no good then, are you young madam? And I'd be quite within my rights to shoot you dead, right here and now.'

'No, please don't.' Una pleaded. 'My mum would be so angry if I made a mess of my new blouse. She hates having to use the hot wash setting, it makes the ironing almost impossible.'

The country gent was unimpressed. 'You have effected an illegal entry and caused criminal damage to the old wisteria, and more too I've no doubt.'

'No, I was only taking a peek through the window to see if it might be the kind of home my parents would like to live in. They're very fussy you know, they hate artexed ceilings, flock wallpaper or anything like that.'

'Intention to effect a break-in to cause criminal damage, or to engage in the theft of property.' The man continued.

'She's as honest as the day's long.' Edward said in Una's defence, although he had no recollection of her parents ever expressing a disliking for artexed ceilings.'

Of course, the man could neither see nor hear Edward and he simply raised the sights of the gun ever so slightly higher and his shoulder stiffened as if readying himself for the gun's recoil.

'And you expect me to believe that load of old codswallop?' He asked.

'I do wish you would.' Una replied and she held her shaking palms together in a position of prayer.

'I tell you now young madam, I'm going to give a count of ten to make good your exit. If you're still in my sights on ten, or if I ever catch you on these premises again, I swear I will blow your brains out. Do you understand?'

Una nodded wildly only because she was too terrified to speak.

'One....' the man began. Una heard no more. She fled back to the point in the wall where the green box awaited her exit and scrambled over heedless of her knees and fingernails, out to the safety of the street.

Chapter 4

Edward had his legs outstretched across the uppermost ridge of the church roof and his back propped against a stone buttress. A dry mouthed gargoyle watched him from a distance its hollow eyes looking out vacantly showing neither interest nor alarm.

'Great views from up here.' Edward said striking up a conversation. 'Not so pretty in the winter, I guess. Freezing gales, eye piercing sleet, skin cracking ice. I guess you've seen it all.'

The gargoyle made no comment and so Edward returned to his thoughts, a regular pastime since he had nobody to talk to. Except Una.

Yet it suited his mood to be up here, high above the town and the noise and the bustle of the street. He could look down to the churchyard below, then across to the row of horse chestnuts and the silvery stream bubbling almost unseen alongside, and watch the afternoon sun reflecting from the wet surfaces.

Then beyond all that the quaint high street with its little row of shops and busy crowds. He tried to recall what it was like to go into a shop, to buy something.

Finally, if he looked hard, the old brick walls of his school were there. His school of former days when he was made to learn.

Yes, he had indeed been doing some serious reflecting about his life and the unusual circumstances in which he found himself, caught as he was between two times each one a hundred years apart. He'd come to a number of important conclusions, the major one being that he wasn't in fact a ghost!

He suddenly jumped out of his skin, startled by the church bells ringing out the hour so close to his ear that he felt their vibrations pulse through his organs and rattle his bones. Three, he counted and then the peace and silence returned. As the chimes faded he spied Una emerging from the great church doors with Nelson pulling impatiently at the lead. He slid on his hands down the grey tiles and made a breathtaking leap from the high buttress to land lightly on the path below.

'You're alive, Una! That's a relief.' He said as he drew level with the girl. Nelson sniffed the air and gave a warning growl.

'Yes, and no thanks to you, Edward. Hardly a knight in shining armour, are you? Melting away like that when I needed rescuing. That nasty crook had me cold in the sights of his gun and could easily have blown my brains out and all you do is leave me there to my fate!'

Edward looked ashamed. 'I'm sorry Una, I don't have any control over myself. One moment I'm here with you and the next I'm back in my own time. It's very frustrating, especially when my best friend is in danger and in need of help.'

'Hmmm.' Una steered The dog through the side gate wishing to avoid the old walled house where he might repeat his stubborn refusal to walk on.

'Are you going to tell the police?' Edward asked.

'No, I'm not. I'm on my way to meet Sebastien and Verity. We always consult together before making decisions. You can join us too if you wish, even if you are a ghost!'

'But I'm not a ghost!' Edward replied indignantly.

'That's an interesting statement considering your recent behaviour.'

'It's complicated, but I've come to an important conclusion about myself.' He continued.

Nelson hurried on and Una increased her stride to match his. 'For a common tram boy you always have such interesting ideas, Edward. Why don't you tell me about it as we walk?'

'Just for the record, I'm not common, Una, as you very well know. In fact, I'm probably the most unique person you're ever likely to meet!'

'You certainly are, Edward! Excuse my teasing, I'm still sore about you abandoning me to my fate in the hands of that armed crook. But tell me anyway, what makes you believe you're not a ghost?'

Edward considered the question.'For certain I'm not, for to be a ghost you have to die first, and I'm still very much alive!'

'Hmmm, then how do you explain how you apparently perished when you tried to recover your toy box from the fire?' Una asked. Memories of the terrible accident in the smoke-filled stockroom still lingered vividly on Una's memory.

'Obviously I did not die!' Edward declared. 'My body was not eaten by flames, burnt or harmed in any way. If you were to prise open the grave below the stone marker in the

churchyard you would find it completely empty and
unused.'

Edward danced a jig to avoid getting tangled in Nelson's
lead then remembered it didn't matter and walked straight
through it instead.

'So how do you explain your existence then, a ghostly waif
invisible to all but me?' Una asked and she threw a ball for
Nelson to chase. When he dropped it back at her feet she
gave him a big hug.

'Good work, Nelson! You're such an intelligent dog!' She
scrubbed the underside of his ears.

'I'm beginning to think of myself more like a traveller in
time!' Edward declared. 'On the day of the fire a lightning
bolt split my existence into two. One part that continues to
exist in a Victorian past, and another, the part which you see
before you now, a splinter, a mere branch of a life that's been
torn away from its trunk by a dreadful calamity.'

'So not so much a ghost as a traveller in time.' Una
observed.

'Yes, something like that.'

'Then welcome Edward, traveller in time and farewell
Edward the ghost!' Una said and gave a polite curtsy of her
skirt and in return Edward removed his grimy neckband
and made a wide bow. Nelson barked, mystified by the
whole ritual.

Soon the school came into view and beyond that the wild
zone with its pond and old oak tree where the friends had
made their den.

As they approached Una spotted Verity and Sebastien
sitting on the bank. Sebastien had his head close to the

water, one hand cupped around a jar and the other raised above it holding a lid ready to catch an insect.

Una took a seat next to Verity and began to tell her about the terrifying encounter with the armed crook. Verity listened wide eyed and shocked with a hand across her mouth.

'Una, we should tell the police, really we must, that armed man could be so dangerous!'

'What's the point, Verity? The crooks are hardly likely to be hanging around waiting to be arrested, are they?' Una felt much braver now the gun barrel wasn't pointed directly at her tender little nose.

'Anyway, calling in the police will surely put a stop to the ghost hunt we have planned for tomorrow and we don't want that to happen do we?'

'Ghost hunt! I can hardly wait!' Sebastien said eavesdropping the conversation.

'We will need to be extra vigilant, Sebastien. Una's had a close encounter with one of the armed crooks she found hanging around the house.'

'Armed crooks?' Sebastien echoed. 'Much scarier than headless ghosts and ghouls, I'm sure, but not really our concern!' His attention seemed to be taken elsewhere.

'What do you have there?' Una asked.

'It's a zebra spider.' He replied. He lifting the inspection jar for her to peer inside.

'Amazing!' Una exclaimed. 'A black and white striped spider, just like a miniature zebra.'

'Except a zebra has only four legs and a spider has twice that number.' Verity interjected.

'Maybe you'll be able to observe it spin a web to catch its prey?' Una said, fascinated as ever by Sebastien's wildlife finds.

'No. The zebra spider doesn't spin a web, it pounces on its prey.'

Verity shuddered. 'A pouncing spider, scary!'

'They also have six eyes which help judge distance when they want to jump on their prey.' Sebastien added with admiration of the creature's attacking prowess.

Nelson came sniffing, jealous of the creature stealing his limelight.

'It's alright, Nelson, we adore you more than any of Sebastien's mini-beasts.' Una reassured him and she gave his brown socked legs a ruffle.

'Actually, the zebra is one of the few spiders you can make friends with!' Sebastien said in defence of the tiny creature. 'If you persevere you can train zebra spiders to take bits of food from your fingers, but you need to work at it to get their trust.'

'No thanks, I'll stick with Nelson. A spider can never be as faithful as a dog. And anyway, whoever heard of anyone taking a spider for a walk?' Una joked.

'Trouble Brews for Band of Bug Hunters.' Verity suddenly exclaimed.

They followed her gaze and saw Mr Pinchcod, the grumpy head teacher striding purposefully in their direction.

'Why are you trespassing on the school grounds, children?' He demanded once within earshot.

'This is our school. We belong here.' Sebastien replied, indignantly.

'No, this is not your school!' The headmaster corrected him. 'The school does not belong to anyone. In fact, you only have a right to be on the premises during normal school hours.'

'This is our after school nature club.' Sebastien lied determined to get the better of him.

'But you are unsupervised. What if you should have an accident, or fall into the pond and drown? What then? You can't expect the teaching staff to be on call all hours of the day and night to be responsible for your safety. Now get off to your own homes immediately.'

Reluctantly the trio trudged away. Una returned Nelson to his lead and while she fiddled with the awkward clip Mr Pinchcod eyed the dog suspiciously.

'Dogs are not permitted in the school grounds,' He stated as if reading from an instructional manual. 'Some dogs are not safe to mix with young people, and often children are intimidated by big dogs like that one. The school management has a responsibility to ensure all our family of pupils feel safe and secure at all times whilst they are in school.'

Mr Pinchcod reached out a hand to give Nelson a pat, but Nelson gave a warning snarl and curled his top lip to display a row of sharp white teeth.

The head swiftly reversed his hand and plunged it deep into a jacket pocket for safety. He began to usher the group through the school gate like a farmer herding sheep. As Sebastien passed the head's eyes suddenly alighted on the inspection jar he held in his palm.

'What do you have there, boy?' He asked.

'It's a zebra spider, sir. I found it on the wall near the pond.'
'Well get rid of it. Creatures living in the grounds are wild and can be dangerous if not handled correctly. Supposing you were bitten and suffered an anaphylactic shock?'
'I've never been shocked in my whole life!' Sebastien retorted.
'But there's always a risk, however small, of an unexpected reaction. You might lose consciousness and die within seconds.' The head warned severely.
'I have a phone to call for help in an emergency.' Verity said waving her tablet at him.
'Too slow!' Mr Pinchcod exclaimed triumphantly. 'You must have a member of the medical team on site, ready to administer an EpiPen jab immediately.' He shook his head and tutted sadly.
The children followed the footpath towards the church walking in a reflective silence as each considered the risks and serious danger they had unwittingly been in.
At last Una broke the silence.
'By the way, Edward claims he's not a ghost after all, but a time traveller and he's trapped in the wrong time. Isn't that so, Edward?' She looked for her friend, but he was gone.
'Hmmm. He must have scarpered when the head showed up, Edward never did like Mr Pinchcod, and still doesn't now despite being invisible!'
Verity and Sebastien smiled politely, they had almost come to terms with Una talking about her old friend as if he were still around.
To change the subject, Verity gave a clap of her hands, 'Beware Ghosts! Tomorrow You Shall Be Hunted Down!'

She exclaimed theatrically, and the gloom was instantly broken by thoughts of what tomorrow promised to bring.

Chapter 5

She met Verity at their agreed rendezvous point the next day. As she arrived she found Verity fiddling with a tiny microphone that she wanted to hide inside her jacket. Eventually she clipped the plastic receiver into place, plugged a fiddly wire into its socket and hid the tablet inside her jacket pocket.

'We can walk along together.' Verity suggested.

'I'd love to, but I have to collect Nelson from the church. And I must call by the bookshop to apologise to Vincent for rushing out last time.'

Verity gave a frown. 'Must you bring that dog with you? The brute will frighten off any ghosts before we even have chance to get up close to them.'

It hadn't occurred to Una that Verity might not be fond of animals, might not adore Nelson as much as she did herself.

'I promised the vicar I'd give Nelson a daily exercise until a home was found for him.' Una apologised. She was meticulous about promises and hated to break one.

'So walk him at another time then. He's not even a member of our club.' Verity complained.

'I like to have him with me. He makes me feel safe.' Una said. It was true, Nelson filled her with confidence whenever they walked together. No crook would dare attempt to steal her satchel while Nelson was by her side.

'He's an unwelcome distraction as far as I'm concerned, Una. I guess I'll have to walk to the house alone and meet you and Sebastien there later.'

So Verity continued onwards to the house while Una diverted to the church.

Verity is jealous! Una said to herself as she collected Nelson from the vestry. She likes to be with me and she needs my company, but I've chosen Nelson ahead of her and now she's jealous and feels rejected.

Friendships could be so difficult at times.

Vincent, by contrast was delighted to make acquaintance with Una's new friend. They became instant pals from the moment Nelson used the bookshop owner's belly as a pillow to snuggle up against.

Vincent was still cross about the rude customers who had insulted him on Una's previous visit. 'It was like being aboard the Marie Celeste.' He complained recalling the way the shop had suddenly emptied. 'One moment the deck was full of customers, the next second, deserted! Everyone had abandoned ship!'

'I'm sorry Vincent, I didn't mean to sneak out like that, but I suddenly remembered I had an important engagement.' Una apologised and sipped the tea he had brought her. She replaced the cup to the table.

'Vincent, do you remember that particular customer, the one who called you Captain Pugwash?'

'I certainly do. I remember every customer who buys a book, but I remember that ignorant beast particularly vividly. I've never been so offended in my whole life!'

'Yes I agree, he was rather unkind! Do you remember the name of the book he bought Vincent?'

'Of course I do. I keep a record of every book I sell.' He flipped out a notepad from his trouser pocket and opened up on a recent entry. 'A History of the Alum Shale Industry at Ravenscar.' He read aloud.

'What a strange choice!' Una exclaimed. 'He didn't look at all like someone who would be interested in history.'

'Yes indeed, I was going to suggest something more along the lines of, 'How to Win Friends and be Popular,' or 'A Dictionary of Insults,' but he didn't look the type to indulge in a joke!'

Una took another sip of her tea thoughtfully. 'Do you know where this Ravenscar place is?' She asked. 'And why would anyone be interested in a history of alum, whatever alum might be?'

'Ravenscar? It's a small village set high on the cliff tops on the coast, about half an hour's drive from here, but I've never heard of any industry going on there. It's just a handful of houses.'

Una was intrigued. She collected Nelson by his lead and apologised again. 'We have to go, Vincent - yet another meeting!'

'Oh well bye then, Una. Ships that pass in the night and all that.'

Una made her way to the rendezvous point on the corner by the green box. She arrived late, out of breath and with Nelson champing at the bit to get inside the grounds. Sebastien already waited there patiently, a ladybird balanced on his fingertip refusing to fly home. Of Verity there was no sign.

'Perhaps she's forgotten about us.' Sebastien suggested.

'No, I spoke to her only an hour ago, she should be here already.' Una told him.

'That is odd, Verity is usually very reliable.' Sebastien said and the ladybird finally made up its mind to soar off home, over the wall.

Una threw her satchel to the pavement and sat on it. She had an inkling that Verity was still annoyed with her about bringing Nelson on the ghost hunt and suspected she might have taken off in a mood.

To while away the time Sebastien began a game with Nelson. It was called, 'show me your paw.' The game was very repetitive but also absorbing; for Sebastien and Nelson at least.

Time passed and daylight slowly began fading to an early evening gloom.

Suddenly Sebastien stopped his game and gave a whistle. 'Hey, take a look at this, Una!' He exclaimed. 'There's a secret pocket in Nelson's collar!'

Sure enough the wide leather band which featured a number of shiny chrome plates, included one with Nelson's name engraved into the metal. Sebastien had discovered this one could be flipped out using a thumbnail. When Sebastien prised his thumb into the top edge a hidden compartment slid open and there snuggly fitting inside the little chamber was a brass door key.

Sebastien picked it out.

'How odd! Why would anyone hide a key in a dog's collar?' Una asked. Sebastien considered the question.

'I have a hunch about that!' He answered thoughtfully. 'Many people get forgetful in their old age, especially with regard to keys. My grandmother was like that. She often locked herself out of the house, or returned home from a

54

shopping trip only to find her door key missing from its usual place. So as an extra precaution, she would hide a spare key underneath a brick close to her front door.'

'That is so true, Sebastien!' Una exclaimed. 'My gran is forgetful too. She uses a length of string with a key attached to one end tied to the inside of her letterbox. Whenever she loses her key all she has to do is push her fingers through the letterbox and pull on the string to get the spare one!'

'So Una, my thinking is this, Nelson's owner, whoever that may be, must also be forgetful, and so keep a spare key locked safely inside Nelson's collar!'

Una's eyes lit up. 'Which means we don't need to break into the house, we can simply use the front door key!' She gasped.

'Exactly so!' Sebastien agreed.

Verity had still not appeared, which was out of character for her.

'I think I may have brought on one of her moods.' Una confessed at last.

'Not exactly hard to do!' Sebastien laughed.

The sky had darkened to purple and night was beckoning so Sebastien decided to write a message for Verity into the dusty top of the green box. 'Gone inside! Catch us there, Sebastien and Una.' It read.

With that done the pair scaled the wall and dropped down into the garden beyond. Meanwhile Nelson leapt the wall with ease and immediately galloped off into the undergrowth.

They had only taken a few steps in the fading light when Una gave a sudden shudder and stopped beside an ivy covered tree stump.

'What's the matter?' Sebastien asked struck by the look of fear in her eyes.

'I'm worried about bumping into the crooks, or the crook with the gun at least.' She admitted. ' I felt safe while Nelson was with us but now he seems to have deserted us.' Sebastien took her by the arm. 'Don't worry Una, I'll stand in front of you and take the bullet.'

'You're such a hero, Sebastien.' Una replied and laughed. If truth be known she did feel reassured by her friend's lighthearted humour in the face of such impending danger. A path led them through tangled branches, probably the route of a local fox, low hanging branches caught their hair to hamper progress in the fading light. Suddenly a black shape darted silently across the purple sky causing a flutter in Una's heart. Sebastien pulled up too, to follow the swift curve of its flight.

'A pipistrel!' He exclaimed. Una breathed again. Bats were creepy but she much preferred those flying ghosts to the spiders whose invisible webs caught in her face and clung to her hair.

She was relieved when they emerged at last from the overgrown grounds to make a sprint across the strip of grass into the cover of the knotty wisteria. Their shadows merging into one under the shade of the house wall.

Una checked back the way they had come and was relieved to note they were unwatched. Only a single light in an old building facing the house was visible, and that was at some distance with the windows shuttered to prevent eyes prying in or out.

The absence of any vehicle on the drive boosted Una's confidence further for she felt certain now that if anybody was inside the house the telltale white van would give away their presence.

'I think we should edge around to the front and try the key.' Una whispered.

Sebastien agreed and led the way keeping tight to the wall to minimise the risk of being seen. But the gravelled drive echoed loudly under their footsteps however lightly they trod and both were relieved when at last the front entrance was within reach.

'Are you sure you're up for this?' Sebastien asked, key at the ready. Una nodded.

He slid the key into the lock and the metal engaged with a nice clean click. A half turn, a twist of the handle and they were inside.

They entered a hallway cloaked in darkness. Without the sense of sight their other senses took over and the first thing Una noticed was the musty odour which hung on the air and the taste of stale plaster which clung to her throat. She gagged and wanted to vomit.

Sebastien clicked a switch down but no light came on. No matter, for after a few minutes their eyes became accustomed to the gloomy scene.

There was a wide corridor leading to a series of closed doors, all painted in the same dull brown which only served to exaggerate the darkness but contrasted starkly against the faded cream walls.

To their immediate right a staircase lead upwards to a second floor above a high ceiling.

'There's nothing to see down here, let's explore upstairs.' Sebastien said and his voice echoed eerily through the empty space.

'I'm annoyed with Verity for not showing.' Una complained as she came to the first step. 'This is a great place for ghost hunting and we don't even have a tablet to record it all.'

'No flashlight either.' Sebastien noted and he tested the wooden handrail.

'She'll have a lot of explaining to do when I catch up with her.' Una continued to rant.

'Una, stop complaining and take a look at this!' Sebastien whispered.

He had reached the foot of the staircase and was carefully inspecting the base of the steps. 'Footprints in the dust, lots of them, leading up and down.'

Looking closely Una could just make out the trail, like tracks in snow, footprints up and down the dusty flight of steps.

'Obviously not supernatural, ghosts don't leave footprints, least of all size ten boot prints!' Sebastien noted.

'Let's take the next level and investigate! ' Una whispered, futile whisperings because the wooden floorboards groaned to their steps so loudly as to forewarn anyone of their upward progress.

Dim shadows jumped from the walls like ghouls, and then appeared to pounce as the two crept in single file up to the next level.

'It's spooky alright, but no blood dripping off the walls, or patches of cold air or any other obvious signs of supernatural activity.' Sebastien observed.

It was almost dark outside now and only a thin sliver of moonlight filtered into the hallway through a high frosted window at the head of the stairs.

'This place must be teeming with the ghosts of former residents. Imagine how many people have lived and died inside these walls since the house was first built.' Sebastien said as he came to the top of the flight.

A corridor mirroring the one on the ground floor now continued straight ahead, again with closed doors leading off on either side.

Sebastien gave each handle a twist as he passed but all were locked, until that is he came to the final door which surprised him when it gave way inward to allow a ray of light to break from the crack.

'Bingo!' He exclaimed.

Una pushed past, impatient to explore and immediately found herself in a large high ceiling room, which may in its heyday have served as a ballroom where dancers and a band might assemble.

A large marble table set in the centre directly below a glass chandelier told Una this was the very same room she had peeked into from the outside balcony the last time she broke into the grounds.

The marble table was still laden with the boxes and containers which Una had seen the crooks unloading, only now there were many more and several chairs had been employed to share the load.

Una was hardly able to hold back her fingers from tearing open the boxes to discover their contents.

'Leave them be, Una. We're ghost hunters remember, not burglars!' Sebastien warned her.

'I don't intend to steal anything.' Una replied curtly. 'I'm only interested in what might be inside.' She felt an almost overwhelming itch to pull open a lid, a curiosity much as Pandora must have felt when that first woman opened the fateful box which unleashed all the evils into the world. Una could no more resist the urge than Pandora and she pulled back the lid of the nearest chest to peer inside.

'Silverware, expensive jewellery and pearl necklaces.' She declared lifting each piece to examine in closer detail.

'This must be the work of a whole tribe of magpies!' Sebastien exclaimed and he too opened the lid of a container. This one held several oil paintings set in gold leaf frames.

'Verity had a hunch the property was being used to store the pickings from local burglaries, and it looks like she was right!' Sebastien said closing the lid.

Una crossed to the window and gazed over the private grounds beyond. Apart from a single light shining in the window of the building on the perimeter all was secluded and still.

'An abandoned house must be the perfect hideaway to store hot property until the heat dies down. Once the trail goes cold the crooks can dispose of it all without causing too much of a stir.' She said to Sebastien.

'And where on earth would you dispose of such a haul of valuable treasures, I wonder?' He replied. 'Every cop in the country must be on the lookout for it, especially locally given the recent spate of robberies in the area.'

'I wish Verity had kept her word. If we had her tablet it would be easy to take photographs to use as evidence. I know stolen property isn't as interesting as ghost related material, but we should still log the finding anyway.' Una said.

'You're right Una. Verity will need to explain herself, but for now I think it's time we made a quick exit. There's no sign of anything supernatural going on in the house and the last thing we need is to be caught red handed by the crooks.'

'Agreed! They obviously intend to return at some point to recover the loot and we don't want to be around when they do!' Una replied.

They were on the point of leaving when Una suddenly stopped dead in her tracks, she put a hand on her friend's arm and exclaimed. 'Sebastien, look at this!'

'What is it?' He asked seeing nothing out of the ordinary. Una picked up a plastic coated wire from under a chair and held it in her fingers.

'I can't be certain, but I think it's an earpiece from Verity's microphone.'

Investigating further, Sebastien bent forward to examine the floor beneath the chair. 'There's something written in the dust.' He announced. 'Several words have been scratched there possibly using a finger.'

'Can you see what the words say?' Una asked.

Sebastien traced the letters using his fingertips. 'They're faint and hard to read but read but it goes something like, 'Kidnap Victim Bound and Gagged by Violent Crooks!'

'And there's been a tussle!' Una exclaimed, for directly beneath the chair legs were numerous scuff marks in the dust.

'Made by shoes being scraped or dragged against the floorboards against their owner's wishes.' Sebastien suggested.

'It must be Verity! She's been abducted, I'm sure of it!' Una cried.

'I think you're right.' Sebastien agreed. 'We must find her before something awful happens.'

They clattered down the stairs heedless now of the noise. Sebastien unlatched the door and bundled through with Una following close behind. Their clumsy feet almost tripped over each other in their headlong rush to escape. But on the threshold they both froze.

The man with the long barrelled gun was waiting there menacingly, aiming the weapon to block their exit. The nightmare scenario which Una had dreaded was become reality.

'So, foolish child, you chose to ignore my well intentioned warning and here you are again, wilfully trespassing on private property. Only this time you have doubled your crime by breaking into the house too.'

'We haven't broken in - I have a key.' Sebastien said and he waved the little metal object in front of the gun barrel, like a magic talisman that might rescue them.

Una was too terrified to reply. The very sight of the weapon caused her whole body to shake uncontrollably. She imagined the little pellet of metal exploding from the cylinder and ripping through her soft flesh scarring her pretty looks forever.

Nor could she suppress the loathing she felt at the man's unkept appearance. He still hadn't washed, shaved or changed his clothing, not once since their last encounter. 'Key or no key, I've had my fill of you miserable young vandals.' The man continued. He lifted the safety cock and his finger curled around the trigger.

Sebastien held up his hands in surrender while Una screeched like a frightened owl. But both actions were lost in a sudden rush of air and a commotion as with the acceleration of a jet plane, Nelson came bounding up from the garden.

In less than a heartbeat the huge beast had arrived at the door and slammed headlong into everyone in his rush to be there.

Una was horrified and afraid the man might suddenly shoot Nelson in order to save himself from being mauled or taken to the ground and horribly savaged.

But nothing so predictable occurred. Instead Nelson jumped up onto the man's chest, wrapped his paws over his shoulders and licked the unshaven face. His short tail wagged furiously in greeting.

'Nelson, heel! Get down, Nelson.' Una commanded as the over exuberant dog continued to slobber over the man almost dragging him to the ground.

'I'm sorry, he's usually really well behaved and obedient.' Una exclaimed in apology.

The man lowered the weapon and said, 'Sit, Nelson!' Immediately the dog took the sitting position. 'Good chap,

Nelson!' The man added in his gruff tones and gave Nelson a pat on his flank.

Una was dumbfounded. 'How on earth do you know Nelson?' She asked incredulously.

'Nelson? Why he's my own dog, how would I not know him!' The man replied. 'But more to the point, how do you know him?'

Una explained how she had been looking after Nelson until his owner was found.

'So you're not a good for nothing vandal after all!'

'And you're not one of the crooks!' Una replied.

'A crook? Not on your life!' He spat out the words with venom. Then his face softened a little and for the first time Una thought she caught the slightest twinkle of warmth in his eyes. 'I think we are going to need to have a chat about things.' He said.

Chapter 6

Saturday morning brought a sharp spring sunlight piercing through the treehouse window where Una and Sebastien met for an emergency meeting.

'We must contact the police and put the investigation into their hands.' Sebastien said. 'We're out of our depth against these crooks.'

'That's certainly true.' Una replied. 'But if we do bring in the police we'll have to explain how we came to be snooping around inside the house. Which could be a bit awkward.'

'Awkward or not, our friend Verity must be in great danger and her life may be at risk if we don't act swiftly.'

As she listened to the wind animating the leaves outside the den's window, Una was thinking about Nelson's owner, Mr Markham. He had warned to steer clear of the house, for their own safety, but promised to tackle the crooks should they return. She hadn't told him of their worries about Verity and how they suspected she must have been abducted.

Her somber thoughts were interrupted by the sound of the wooden ladder blocks clattering noisily against each other. Somebody was climbing up causing the steps to swing wildly from side to side.

'It must be Verity! She's safe!' Una exclaimed. For who else could it be climbing into their secret Eyrie?

But it was not Verity. Instead Aunt Aggie's face appeared in the doorway her clammy hands groping for a hold. Her bob of grey hair was followed by a barrelled torso and then two sausage legs which splayed from side to side forcing

Sebastien and Una to duck this way and that to avoid being flattened.

At last the old caretaker lay inside panting on the boards. 'Suffering sparrows, that nearly killed me.' She wheezed through rattling lungs. 'What on earth made you build a nest in a storming great tree?'

'It's designed to deter unwanted visitors.' Una explained causing the old caretaker to frown and she had to make a rapid apology.

'But you're always welcome, auntie Aggie.' She assured her.

'Don't worry, I don't think I'll be making a return visit, not after the trauma I've suffered this time; once bitten twice shy as the saying goes.' She looked back down the length of rope. 'And I've still to get down yet, which might prove the death of me!'

'Going down is easy, Aggie. You just lower yourself a rung at a time.' Sebastien said.

'As it happens, I wasn't planning on abseiling down!' Aggie replied with a cheeky grin. 'Anyway, the thing I want to know is, what are you two mischief makers plotting up here in the clouds at this unearthly hour of the morning?'

Una and Sebastien's eyes met in silent agreement to come clean, to confide in Aggie and tell her the truth.

'We're in a fix Aunt Aggie.' Sebastien told her.

'Verity's been kidnapped by violent thugs.' Una continued. She wasn't absolutely sure they were violent crooks, but it felt right to anticipate a worst case scenario.

Sebastien told Aggie about the ghost hunt, how they had discovered the stash of stolen property and the secret mayday message written in the dust.

'Verity must have been captured while she was investigating the house and now the crooks are probably holding her hostage to prevent her squealing to the police.' Una said.

'And now we can't decide what to do next.' Sebastien told her.

'You mustn't tell the police!' Aggie warned. 'The crooks will be spurred into desperate measures if they know the law is closing in on them.'

'But we must do something!' Una protested.

'Have they sent you anything through the post?' Aggie asked.

Una and Sebastien returned mystified looks. 'No!' They declared.

'Good. Sometimes crooks cut off a finger of their victim and post it in an envelope if they need to prove the hostage is still alive.'

Una held a hand over her mouth to stifle a scream. 'That's awful!' she exclaimed.

'The situation isn't desperate. Not yet. But we do need to act fast. Do you have any idea where the crooks might have taken Verity?' Aggie asked.

'None.' Sebastien answered. But Una suddenly remembered her chance meeting with the gang in Vincent's bookshop. 'One of them bought a book about the history of some old alum works at Ravenscar. Vincent says it's a village on the coast, but I've never heard of the place.'

'If it's the only lead we have, then we must check it out. I'll get the car.' Aggie declared. She rolled over and lowered herself awkwardly down the precarious ladder before landing in a heap at the base.

'Get the car?' Sebastien mouthed in astonishment.

'I didn't even know she could drive!' Una replied.

They slid down the ladder, skirted the pond and waited by the school entrance.

Moments later a plume of dirty smoke came billowing down the tarmac accompanied by the deep growl of an engine and a stench of burning oil.

Out of the smoke like in a B rated movie there appeared a battered old jeep, painted in a dull khaki green and topped with matching canvas roof. It pulled up at the kerb with a screech of the brakes and the passenger side door was thrown open.

'Climb in!' Aggie ordered from the driver's seat.

Sebastien jumped into the worn leather passenger seat allowing Una to shuffle past him into the cramped space behind the driver and they were ready to go!

Aggie's skills as a caretaker obviously didn't transfer to the maintenance of her own vehicle. The windows were splattered with mud and the leather seats littered with oily rags, half empty cans, and bottles filled the floor, but none of these seemed to affect the old vehicle's workings, for off they sped at breakneck speed with Aggie wrestling the oversized steering wheel and clunking through the gears. Soon they were headed out to the coast, up high over the clifftop roads with a playful gale rattling through gaps in the roof and a sharp salty air pinging off their nostrils.

The road shrank to a single track for the final few miles, twisting and looping between hill and hedgerow. Vehicles travelling in the opposite direction were forced to swerve hastily onto the verge to allow the old jeep to pass.

When eventually the track came to an abrupt end Aggie flipped up a window and leaned her head through the gap to hail a passing dog walker. 'Excuse me lovey, we're looking for the Adam works?'

'You mean the Alum works? Follow the path it's on the right.' The walker pointed towards the edge.

Una prepared to bail out, but Aggie hit the accelerator and threw the wheel sharply to the left. The jeep crashed heavily over a high kerb setting the cabin rolling to and fro like a ship in a storm.

After a few more metres Aggie applied the handbrake and they were all relieved to disembark. Una gazed out towards the cliff edge, facing seaward where the skeletal foundations of a small village had once stood.

The outlines of one building were huge, perhaps the size of a swimming pool, but the others were much smaller, possibly the remains of simple industrial units or the dwellings of worker families.

Turning her eyes from the sea, Una noticed that a massive gash had been bitten away from the cliff almost as if a dinosaur had made lunch of the rock leaving behind the grey-white chalky intestines exposed to the elements.

The only sign of modern life came from a wooden information hut out in the distance, where brightly coloured flags flapped from a tall mast.

Aggie rested her arms on her hips and frowned across the barren landscape. 'No sign of young Verity here, folks. You'd better take a scout around while I check the oil. This old beast drinks it like tea!' She lifted the rusty bonnet and immediately began tinkering about inside.

Una and Sebastien split in opposite directions, north and south to cover as much ground as possible.

The sharp wind tugged at Una's black hair and billowed out her skirt. Framed by the inky sky and grey sea she had the appearance of a waif child, the ones you see in old oil paintings, a lost soul in a barren landscape.

She soon found herself picking a way through ancient stone foundations, loose brickwork and jagged rock walls. At the farthest end from her there arose a neat circle of brickwork, the base of a tall chimney perhaps, but now merely a blunt stump with ivy and blue flowered speedwell scrambling up its lichen stained surface.

Wandering down further Una reached the beginnings of a railway track leading away towards the cliff edge. Judging by the deeply worn tracks the line probably dated from a similar age to the old stone foundations.

Not much call for a railway service here, Una noted to herself. She cleared some weeds to reveal more of the track. Probably not a passenger line at all then, but one to carry the wagons needed to shift heavy rock from one place to another.

Una's mind wrestled over the question of how Verity's fate at the hands of the crooks could possibly be connected to this old alum works on a remote headland.

Suddenly Sebastien rushed up absolutely bursting with excitement. Una's hopes rose assuming he must have found Verity.

'Look at what I've found!' He exclaimed and he opened his palms to reveal a small reptile nestled inside. 'It's a common lizard, a male judging by the red underside. I caught him sunbathing on the rocks. I guess the spring sunshine must have stirred him out of hibernation.'

Una gave a groan. 'Verity is in mortal danger and all you can think about is hunting reptiles among the rocks!'

Sebastien was shamefaced and returned the lizard to an exposed section of wall.

'To be fair, Una, I did look, but couldn't find anything of interest. Unless you count a locked shed near to the quarry face. Shall we take a look at it?'

Una had no better plan so she allowed Sebastien to lead her across more foundations until they arrived at a secure brick building the size of a garden shed, the type used to store tools or machinery. A wagon rested on a track nearby.

The building had a padlocked door and a small rectangular window blanked over with a steel shutter.

'I'd like to know what's inside.' Sebastien said and he gave the lock a tug but it was securely fastened.

'It may be railway equipment.' Una replied. 'I have a feeling a track began here and led down to the works closer by the cliff.'

They followed the track as it weaved a course between the old foundations before descending away steeply and coming to an abrupt end on the very brink of a vertical drop.

Leaning into the wind Sebastien caught sight of a beach far below, a tiny triangle of sand bordered by craggy rocks and white crested waves which from such a distance rushed up silently on the shore.

'This is the quick route down to the beach.' Sebastien quipped. 'A ten second flight followed by a sudden crash landing and the worst headache imaginable.'

'It's not funny, Sebastien. We're no closer to finding Verity and we still have no idea how these old ruins or the railway might be connected to her whereabouts, or the thieves who kidnapped her!'

'You're right Una. I think we may be on a wild goose chase.' Sebastien agreed.

'Maybe I need to take a walk along the cliff to think things out, and maybe clear my head of all this fog.' Una said and she set off alone along the cliff path.

She set out at a brisk pace at first, but after a few hundred metres the path began to descend sharply down a steep incline forcing her to be ever more cautious with her footing.

Eventually the rough track turned into a series of unevenly eroded steps which weaved right and left between rocky outcrops always downwards, always towards the distant sea.

She made slow progress but the beach crept ever closer and the growl of the sea grew ever louder. Waves moved rhythmically in and out like a breathing monster.

Now as she came to the base of the cliff the rough steps had eroded away completely so that Una found herself travelling the last few metres scrambling on hands and knees, edging herself cautiously over points where a slip might cause a nasty tumble down the bank.

Thoughts of a broken collar bone or dislocated ankle in such a remote place filled her with horror and so it was with much relief that her feet came at last to rest on the firm triangle of sand where sea met land.

Now the cliff face loomed dark behind her, a giant barrier which blocked out the warmth of the sun.

A colony of seals, perfectly camouflaged against the sand honked noisily when Una inadvertently approached too close into their territory.

The strenuous descent had left her exhausted so Una lay herself on a bed of dry rock with beads of sweat glistening on her forehead and more than a tinge of peach blushing her cheeks. She closed her eyes and listened to the orchestra of waves and the terse cries of hungry gulls.

Some time later when she reopened her lids she found Edward sitting close by, looking out to sea.

'There's a kind of peace here at the bottom of the cliffs.' He said. Something in the regular rush of the waves.'

Una sat up and combed the knots from her hair.

'No ghosts to haunt you down here then?' Una asked.

'Look around you, Una.' Edward replied. At first she saw nothing, but then she found almost hidden between tall pillars of rocks the rusting remains of a shipwreck. Stained lines of rivets and the hollow shell of a steel hull, waging war against the constant thrash of salty water and the cutting winds.

'Ghosts here too then, the ghosts of drowned sailors, I guess?' Una said.

'Ordinary people hear the cry of gulls, but I hear the cry of ghosts.' Sebastien replied. 'Not just sailors but the cry of children too, the cries of a boy and a girl trapped on a beach.
'That must be terrifying!' Una cried in shock.
'I have something interesting to show you, Una. Follow me.' He led to a tiny cove where a section of the cliff had been carved away to form a small hollow and fitting snugly inside was a worn stone marker with two names cut into it. Over a hundred years or more the sea had slowly washed away the letters until they could no longer be distinguished. 'I can usually put such things to the back of my mind, but down here I hear the insistent cry of those two young children tugging at my conscience and for some reason I can't ignore them. I think they may need my help, but I don't know how or why.'
Una told Edward about Verity's disappearance in the room of stolen goods. 'So there are two mysteries for us to solve then. The kidnapping of Verity....'
'...And the problem of the two ghost children.' Edward finished the sentence for her.
The sea was creeping in all around unnoticed.
'Talking of Verity.' Una continued, 'While I've been resting here with my eyes closed I may have hit upon the link between the stolen goods in the old house and the alum industry here on the coast.'
'Tell me, Una, I'm all ears!' Edward pleaded.
'Two hundred years ago roads were so rough and potholed that the best way to move goods from one place to another was by boat.' She began.

'And boats were able to carry much heavier loads than could be carried by road.' Edward suggested.

'Yes, I'm sure that's so.' Una agreed.

'But I still don't understand how Verity and the stolen goods come into it.' Edward complained.

'Verity believed the crooks were storing their haul in the 'safe house' until the heat had died down. She said every officer in the country was on the lookout for stolen goods because of the recent spate of robberies. The press and papers were full of news about them too.'

'Too risky to offload the stuff at a local antique centre then?' Edward guessed.

'Exactly! So the crooks needed to store their thefts in an empty house until the heat dies down, then dispose of it far away where no one has heard about the robberies.'

'Like in another country?' Edward guessed.

'Right again, Edward!'

Una climbed down from the rock and moved further inland. The tide was flooding onto the beach now, splashing over her legs and encircling the rocks to form ever shrinking islands.

'Getting the stolen goods out of the country is a great plan except for one big problem. The customs! Every port will be on high alert just as the police are. They'd soon sniff out anything suspicious being transported in the crooks' baggage.' Una had to move again, closer to the wall of cliffs. 'But let's suppose the crooks found a way of sneaking the valuables out to a remote part of the coast where they could easily be smuggled abroad on a small boat.'

'Of course, that's amazing, Una!' Edward said, suddenly seeing the light.

'And everything is going smoothly until one nosy kid happens to discover the stolen goods while hunting for ghosts!'

Edward snapped his fingers. 'So they have to kidnap the kid to stop her squealing to the police! Suddenly everything makes sense.'

Una hesitated now to look darkly across to Edward.

'Only, once the stolen goods are safely out of the country the crooks will have no further use for their hostage, so they'll have to dispose of her. And my guess is it won't be pretty.' She concluded.

But when she looked up Edward had vanished. She was alone on the beach with the family of astonished seals.

Una suddenly became aware of the tide rushing in fast all around her.

She scanned the cliff-face searching for the path which had led her to the beach, but menacing shadows of the encroaching afternoon had distorted her bearings and her sense of direction faltered.

Panic set in.

The only alternative to the cliff path was a five mile hike along the rapidly disappearing beach, over to Robin Hood's Bay. With the tide rushing in towards her she faced the imminent danger of being swept out to sea where she would surely drown in the cold waters.

With no alternative, Una began to run towards her only hope of salvation, the distant village with the waves already nipping at her ankles and flooding over her feet.

Soon her shoes began to drag like sodden weights on her ankles and she was compelled to remove the unwieldy fashion accessories, but now the sharp rock cut into the soles of her tender feet and stones stubbed at her soft pink toes making them raw and painful.

With pounding heart Una fled, heedless of the pain and discomfort until with a sob of relief she happened upon a fissure in the cliff wall, a place where the shale had eroded and collapsed onto the beach forming a steep diagonal escape path, an emergency exit from the sea.

Here she was able to scramble on hands and knees like an animal and slowly edge her way up to the safety of the high alum track.

After a long trek in the late afternoon heat she finally arrived back at the jeep, breathless and sore and a mere shadow of her usual immaculate self. Her wet skirt clung like a towel to her ankles and her white blouse was splattered with streaks of sticky brown soil from her slips and tumbles in the boggy ground.

Most distressing of all, she found that her delicate nails had been chaffed and scuffed from clutching desperately at the abrasive rock during her panic stricken scramble up the slope.

She found Aggie asleep at the wheel, her swollen legs bent across the steering wheel, her head lolled against the driver side window. She was snoring contentedly.

At first Sebastien was nowhere to be found, but then a sudden darting movement in the heather drew her attention and there he was, leaping from side to side in a strange zig-zag dance. Una immediately called him over.

'I was looking for adders.' He explained. 'They come out of hibernation about this time of year and you can often find them sunbathing on warm rocky shelves.'

'Trust you to seek out every living creature within a ten mile radius but not find a single trace of Verity!' Una snapped. She had come to the end of her tether!

She gave Aggie a shake to return the snoring giant back to the land of the living. They would have to return home, empty handed.

'Looks like we have to admit defeat.' Una bemoaned to the blurry eyed caretaker.

'The only place she might be hidden is in the shed over there, but it's more secure than Fort Knox.' Sebastien noted. Aggie said she'd like to check it out before they left.

Being a long serving school caretaker, she had acquired a whole range of essential skills needed to deal with the seemingly never ending range of duties she faced from day to day. Rescuing footballs from dangerous rooftops, improvising her broom handle to fend off rabid dogs on the playground, or deploying restraining techniques while releasing a child's head from the school railings all featured in her vast arsenal.

The doughty caretaker took one look at the steel shuttering and declared, 'I think we can prise open this little can of worms, no messing.'

She reversed the jeep to the window then rooted about in the boot compartment and found a towing chain. She clamped one end to the jeep and the other to the steel shutter.

'Stand well clear - this could be messy!' She warned and jumped into the driver's seat. The huge wheels began to creep slowly forward and the chain took up the slack. It strained ominously as the metal drew taught then gave a dangerous hum as the four wheels locked hard against earth.

A stench of burning clutch oil filled the air and for an awful second both engine and steel shutter were locked in a duel of strength. But there was only to be one winner and the contest lasted only a matter of seconds before the shutter surrendered with a painful scream of metal rivets exploding outwards from their housing. They squealed like pigs as they pinged out with the velocity of bullets. With a sickening crack the whole sheet suddenly exploded outwards from its bracket and the jeep bounded forward like a kangaroo.

'Yahoo! You cracked it, Aggie!' Sebastien shouted in excitement and he immediately leapt forward to poke his head through the newly revealed opening.

At first the space inside seemed full of gloom and darkness, but once his eyes had adjusted he whistled in astonishment. The chamber was filled with what appeared to be a nest of giant insect eggs. Massive pill shaped eggs, each one an unblemished white, piled one on top of another, a pyramid of immense larvae.

Sebastien half expected to come face to face with some monstrous adult ant jealously guarding her clutch.

'What on earth are they?' Una asked peering through herself.

By way of answer Sebastien shinned up the ledge and lowered himself inside.

Once amongst the eggs his theory of a brood of monstrous insects was quickly crushed.

'They're large plastic containers of some sort.' He said running his fingers along the smooth edges.

'They're quite light with a joint down the centre where the two halves clip together. I'll break one open if I can find the clip.'

His fingers groped around the middle and soon found the trigger, a spring loaded clip which he soon released with a sharp click.

'Got it! Like breaking an egg in two!' Sebastien exclaimed and the capsule split apart.

But there was no living yoke inside, no slimy albumen, no dormant worm awaiting a welcome release into the world, only a vacant, hollow space.

'Try another.' Una urged.

Sebastien unclipped a second and then a third each time with similar results, the opened shells forming a heap of cracked eggs on the floor but disappointingly with nothing of interest hidden inside.

'Not as exciting as I had imagined.' Sebastien declared sadly like a child who discovers the Easter egg he has dreamt of cracking open for weeks turns out to be hollow.

More than that, Sebastien would dearly have loved to discover a colony of an entirely new insect species, giant ants or wasps, warm and ready to hatch. How amazing would that be!

But his disappointment was short lived for at that moment he heard a faint knocking coming from a capsule he hadn't yet broken apart.

'It's the one at the back.' Una shouted from the window. 'Pull it down to look inside.'

This one proved much heavier than the first and Sebastien struggled to lower the slippery case to the floor. He didn't want to accidentally crack the egg open and spill its contents on the hard concrete floor.

Once safely on the ground he soon got to work to release the spring and the white capsule broke cleanly in two. There, fitted snuggly inside was Verity, hands and legs tied and a length of sticky tape across her mouth.

With shaking hands Sebastien untied her wrists then roughly ripped off the tape. Verity drew a deep breath and let out an ear splitting scream, a scream of pain, a scream of joy at being released from the dark and cramped cell.

'Sweet Freedom and Fresh air! Rejoice!' She yelled as she stretched out her arms in relief.

Chapter 7

Una passed beneath the gothic archway into the cool interior. She found the vicar under the tower, busy as he always was, this time peeling and cutting vegetables for the soup kitchen.

His long fingers made a well practised twist of the cutter blade, dipped the potato in fresh water, then repeated the movement times with a practiced ease. Peelings mounted up on the wooden trestle table; spirals of carrot, parsnip and dull red squash.

The black brows lifted as Una approached and he greeted her warmly without fingers straying from their important task.

'Good morning, Una. You'll have to excuse me working while we chat, lunch must not be delayed, for the masses will not tolerate poor service where food is concerned!'

Una's eyes stretched across the empty spaces between the rows of ornate stone arches and upwards to the high roof. She felt as always belittled by contrast to the awesome architecture.

'Thank you so much for finding Nelson's owner!' The vicar continued in his cheerful voice. 'Mr Markham was so pleased to be re-united with his faithful pet and to have him returned safely home.'

Una had been expecting to give Nelson his morning walk and was dismayed to find her companion no longer there. 'When did he go?' She asked.

'Mr Markham dropped by to collect him yesterday evening. He was full of praise for you Una, told me how he had stumbled on you and your friend outside his employer's empty house.'

'Sebastien and I were doing a little exploring.' Una explained.

'I think Mr Markham was concerned that he'd frightened you. He was on the lookout for burglars you see, and thought you were up to no good.'

The vicar emptied the skinned vegetables into a large blackened cauldron of hot water and sat it on a portable hob behind the table. He dried off his fingers to add several spoonfuls of herbs, salt and black pepper to the pot.

'Anyway, I reassured him you were a most trustworthy individual and not at all as might be expected from your outward appearance.'

Una smiled briefly, unsurprised by the assumption made on the basis of her choice of clothing.

She thanked the vicar for his kind words then left without further delay. She had suddenly experienced an uncomfortable sense of loss, an aching in the pit of her stomach brought about by the unexpected absence of her loyal friend. She felt like a bereaved mother.

Wandering listlessly across to the stone marker she settled down on her leather satchel by the grass verge. In nostalgic mood she savoured the cool morning air.

Early blossom set loose by a light breeze floated lazily down from the row of cherry trees, like pink snowflakes. A scattering came to settle softly in her raven hair while others chose to polka dot her blouse and black skirt.

'You look a picture!' Edward observed, and Una's black eyes twinkled at the sudden appearance of her ghost friend. She needed his company right now.

'Or an oil painting, perhaps.' The boy continued. 'You know, one of those sentimental images you find on the lids of biscuit tins or boxes of chocolates.'

'You can stop right there, Edward. I am not getting romantically entangled with a ghost!'

Edward laughed. 'Come on, Una, where's your sense of adventure?'

'Especially not a poorly dressed ghost with a hygiene problem!' She continued unimpressed by Edward's taunting.

Sometimes it irked Una, or saddened her to see her friend dressed in the same dirty shirt and oil stained trousers every day without ever washing. Even the handkerchief knotted around his neck showed signs of sweat marks and engrained dirt. But today it didn't matter so much.

'I've told you, I'm not a ghost.' Edward replied.

'Then traveller in time or whatever it is you claim to be.' Una corrected herself.

'It is truly so, I am indeed a traveller in time and I duly confess to it.' Edward grinned.

'You're beginning to sound like a circus showman!' Una said and Edward bowed theatrically before her.

'You see, a true ghost is forever condemned to haunt the one same spot, trapped as they are in a particular moment of time, usually in the place where some dreadful life ending tragedy occurred.'

84

'As when you perished in the smoke while rescuing your box of toys?' Una asked recalling the terrible accident he had suffered.

'Yes, exactly! 'Edward replied. 'But in my case a unique and almost magical transformation took place in that moment. My body was not burnt, but instead released into the air allowing my essence to roam freely in time and space.'

'Only almost magical?' Una echoed.

Edward took a leap and a somersault in the air then landed squarely on the tiled roof of a well where visitors drew their water to quench thirsty flowers and refresh the dogs that accompanied them to the cemetery.

'Of course, nearly magical.' He said balancing on the tiles. 'I'm hardly a Peter Pan, am I? Just look at me, a common tram boy from a working class family standing here before you as large as life.' He gave a low bow then jumped down to rejoin Una.

'In escaping unscathed from the horrors of that smoke filled room I ceased to be a ghost. The Edward, as you knew him then ceased to be, but by some strange twist of fate this essence of my former self has become a free spirit, a traveller between times.'

Una drew the battered old toy from her satchel. 'Do you remember when you disappeared without a trace and without a goodbye? You left me this present of a lead soldier. I always keep it with me, in case one day you never return.'

'You're such a sop, Una!' Edward teased, but Una ignored the lighthearted comment.

'I think being caught between different times must be very frustrating for you Edward, and you must be very bored here with only me to talk to.'

Una returned the toy to her satchel and smiled. 'But on the other hand, it is wonderful to have you as my friend. Even if you do stink of horse manure.'

'That's very funny, Una!'

'Yes it is, but seriously, I think you must miss the noise and bustle of the trams and the company of the horses and your entire family while you're here in the future with me.' Una continued.

Edward concentrated his thoughts in order to answer this difficult question.

'It's very odd, but I'm beginning to believe that time is rather like one of those carousel rides you find at a fairground. Always in motion, always turning. Only I seem to have found a way of jumping on and off the ride.

No matter how long I spend with you, when I return to my Victorian family, time seems to have stood still. It's as if I jump off the carousel at a point in time to visit you then when I jump back on I find myself at exactly the same spot as when I jumped off. It's like time stands still in the other place while I'm gone.

'That is such an interesting idea, Edward.' Una declared. 'When you grow old and wise I feel sure you are destined to become one of the great thinkers of our age, someone like Stephen Hawkins.'

'Thank you Una. The only problem is that I don't have any control over when I jump on and off! It's all very odd!'

Bells rang out the hour and a sudden breeze shook blossom from the row of trees causing a ripple of blossom to shiver through the air in a rhythmical dance mimicking the music of the bells.

'But that's not all, Una.' Edward continued enthusiastically now that he'd set out on the journey. 'I'm like an infant of time, an innocent child with a thirst for knowledge about my situation. Every day I discover more about my capabilities and what I'm able to achieve!'

'For example, yesterday after our meeting at Ravenscar, I found that if I put my mind to it, I can actually travel back to any other time in the past!'

Una was perplexed. 'You told me your life had become splintered into two parts, this one which you are dragged into randomly, and the Victorian one where you live out the main part of your existence?'

'And that is as I believed, but yesterday evening I found myself once again by the cliffs at the alum works.'

Una was not impressed and folded her arms crossly. 'You were obviously more taken with the place than I! My shoes were ruined, my dress soaked in brine and my blouse irreversibly stained with mud! And that's not to mention my broken nails and grazed toes and ankles.'

Una had spent several hours making emergency repairs but it would take many months before her nails were restored to their former level of perfection.

'Worst of all, you abandoned me and left me stranded on a remote beach!' Una continued, her voice rising to a crescendo.

Edward looked shocked. 'Did I really? As usual, I'm full of remorse, Una!'

'And so you should be.' She scolded. 'But never mind, you know, spilt milk and all that, even though I hate the place I'm still dying to know more about your visit to Ravenscar.' Edward gathered in his legs and took a seat astride his own stone marker.

'The truth is I was so intrigued by the two ghost children who I heard crying on the beach at the base of the cliffs that I felt compelled to find out more about them.'

A bright-eyed grey squirrel scampered across the grass, paused a second at the base of the tree to observe the strange girl talking to herself then continued upwards in a helter-skelter race around and round the trunk only stopping once it had reached the topmost branch.

Regaining Una's attention, Edward continued the story of his return to the alum works.

'I needed to know why the two children were haunting the cliffs in such a sorrowful state and what catastrophe had caused them to perish so young in life.'

'And did you find your answer?' Una asked.

Edward stalled. 'The strange thing is, as I strode down to the alum works I quickly realised that the site was altered dramatically since my last visit. In fact I had unknowingly travelled back in time some two hundred years!'

Una looked unconvinced. 'So you went there yesterday, but in reality you had travelled back two hundred years. How may I ask did you know? Do you have a time travel device to warn you? Like, welcome guest, you have now arrived in the year 1820!'

Edward laughed. 'No, nothing so clever as that. I knew because the alum work buildings were almost new, carved from freshly cut stone and brick, not ancient remains and foundations as they are today. And there were people everywhere, busy at their work, and the air was filled with the sound of voices and the noises of industry.'

Una's expression suddenly became earnest. 'And did you find the ghost children?' She asked.

'I believe I did.' He confirmed. 'A girl and her brother, both innocently at play directly outside the door to their home.'

'So the dreadful event or accident had not occurred at that point in time when you arrived?' Una guessed.

'It had not.' Sebastien agreed. 'And that's what started me thinking. Supposing I was able to change their history? Imagine if I could use my ability to travel in time to somehow prevent the awful accident whatever it was, from occurring?

If I was able to alter their histories and allow them to enjoy full lives, to become mature adults instead of being cut off short in their infancy. How amazing would that be?'

Chapter 8

Una felt at ease with the world after the rescue of Verity from the strange insect cell. No impending danger hung over her, no sword of Damocles, she was able to relax into the gentle routine of school life.

Of course, the mystery of the burgled goods and the crooks' connection with the alum works still played on her mind, but Una did take comfort in the knowledge that her friend at least was safe.

Verity herself seemed untroubled by her terrifying experience. Meeting in the Eyrie she calmly recalled events leading up to her capture as Una and Sebastien listened on in shocked silence.

It seems she had intended to show off, to prove herself capable of hunting ghosts unaided, without the support of her friends, but rather than ghosts she had stumbled upon the stolen goods.

She panicked, suddenly aware of her vulnerability, a young girl alone in an unfamiliar house. So she had clattered headlong down the stairs right into the arms of Tinker, the woman and a couple of 'heavies' as she called them.

After a heated debate the crooks had decided to drive her down to the coast where they locked her inside one of the insect pods. Verity had no inkling of what fate they had in mind for her, but guessed it would not be pleasant. They each vowed never again to go out on a limb, but always to stay together, with strength as a team.

Back on the main street Una's heart lightened further in the sparkle of fresh spring sunshine. Everywhere a razor sharp light danced and dappled across the scene with bursts of intense lemon and pink from the rows of cherry trees set alongside the road.

She passed the little bookshop where Vincent lounged in the window and gave a friendly wave but the bookshop owner was preoccupied, daydreaming about the sea no doubt and unaware of her presence.

A pang of guilt swept through her as she recalled the rushed exit of her previous visit and she made a mental note to drop in whenever the next opportunity arose.

For now she was happy to swing her satchel across a shoulder, cross at the Belisha and head down the church cutting to meet her day in school.

The morning dragged on, such was normality. Una coasted through the daily mathematics and English lessons and by lunch had no memory of anything she'd been taught, or whether the work had been interesting or even challenged her.

But in the afternoon an incident occurred which left a dark stain on her memory which was not so easily forgotten.

It happened while she worked with Verity in the classroom library, a quiet corner within the classroom where pupils were free to study from project books or a computer, usually to find out about an aspect of history, science or sometimes geography.

Under this pretence the pair had been looking for information about Ravenscar and the history of the nearby alum works. Verity had drawn a rough sketch of the coastline and marked in the positions of the alum buildings on the high cliff while Una traced the routes of the boats which sailed from the beach below to ports such as Hull and Newcastle.

They worked in a relaxed style away from the usual bustle of the class and without the close supervision of a teacher. There was time to chat amiably to pass the time and as Una turned the pages of a book she scribbled down notes in her jotter.

'As if it wasn't challenge enough to cut the shale from the cliff-face using simple tools like picks and shovels, the workers then had to burn the shale on a huge bonfire. Often the flames burnt for nearly a year before they could extract the precious alum from the ashes.'

'Even then the backbreaking work wasn't complete for they had to somehow shift the heavy blocks of crystal down from the high cliff to a waiting boat.' Verity said, reading from a page in the book.

'Yes, the cliffs were a big problem!' Una agreed recalling the miserable day she had spent scrambling down the steep path and the drama of her scramble up the shale landslide to avoid being cut off by the incoming tide.

Their conversation was suddenly interrupted by Sebastien who came barging through the classroom door and almost skittled over the table and its contents in his breakneck haste.

'Verity! Hide quickly! There's someone coming who you don't want to meet!' He cried in alarm and in the next instant Mr Pinchcod marched into the classroom closely followed by two adults.

For once it wasn't the bad tempered headmaster whose arrival Sebastien was giving advance warning of but rather the man and woman who followed behind him. Una immediately recognised the man by the distinctive patch covering one eye, and the woman by her tight red lips and stiff meringue-like hairstyle.

'Oh no, it's the crooks!' Una whispered and Verity quickly dived beneath the desk, for Tinker would surely recognise her as the girl he had caught in the old house and bundled inside an insect pod.

Sebastien quickly stole into Verity's seat and rested his legs over her back hoping in that way to conceal her. Verity gave a squeal of pain.

'Stay still and quiet, Verity.' Una hushed her.

'Don't let them lock me up in that pod again!' Verity pleaded back in a distressed croak.

'Lay still and we'll hide you until they've gone!' Sebastien told her.

Mr Pinchcod led the visitors to the front desk where Una's teacher was sat marking books. Una pretended to be writing in her jotter while at the same time eavesdropping in on the conversation which ensued.

'Good morning, Ms Bateson.' The head greeted the teacher.

'A pleasure to see you and your pupils working so industriously as always.' Mr Pinchcod beamed a gracious smile across the sea of busy children.

'Allow me to introduce you to our very important visitors, this is Mr Smith and this, Mrs Smith.'

Ms Bateson offered each a polite smile.

'The Smith's have recently moved into the area and are looking for a school for their daughter. They're hoping to secure one with the high educational standards which they and their daughter desire.'

The headmaster made a flourish with outspread palms to encompass the busy children. 'I'm sure we will be able to fulfil their needs admirably.'

The visitors took in the scene, the tidy arrangement of desks, the engaging displays, shelves of books and the abundant pots of pencils, paper and coloured crayons adorning the tops of cupboards.

Both seemed eager to mingle among the class and Mr Pinchcod sensing their impatience invited the visitors to explore the class freely as they wished.

'The best indicator of a successful school is always to be found in its pupils!' He declared proudly. 'So please do ask the pupils any questions or queries you may have.'

Una eyed the pair with suspicion as they began to circulate around the desks. On the one hand she felt confident they would not remember her from their brief encounter in the bookshop, but on the other she was certain Verity would be instantly recognised as the girl they had kidnapped. She drew her chair closely into the table to hide as best possible her friend crouched beneath.

Tinker approached from one direction while the woman made a pincer movement closing in from the other. Una couldn't help notice that while they passed rapidly by the tables of boys, hardly giving each face a passing glance, when they came to a table of girls they stopped longer and studied each face intently.

They're searching for Verity! The thought suddenly struck Una and a cold shudder ran down her spine.

If she had believed the crooks might have cut their loses and forgotten about the troublesome girl who had escaped their clutches, she was very much mistaken. Here they were hot on her trail!

For the first time now Una pictured in her mind the moment when the crooks returned to discover the secure metal panels ripped away from their hinges and the girl they had imprisoned missing. How their ire and anger must have burned at being so embarrassingly undermined by mere children.

Now they had penetrated the seemingly safe school environment to sniff out their former captive and to identify those responsible for setting her free.

Presumably they intended to inflict some kind of horrible revenge upon them. Una's mind reeled with the unpleasant images of what the crooks might intend should they succeed.

Soon Mr and Mrs Smith, as they called themselves, arrived in the library area where Sebastien and Una pretended to study and where Verity hid below with eyes tightly closed and fingers crossed.

They were closely monitored by Mr Pinchcod who had followed the visitors around the classroom taking a keen interest in anything his pupils had to say to them.

'Good afternoon, children.' The woman said in greeting, displaying a broad white smile which stretched almost up to her artificial eyebrows. 'What wonderful work you are engaged in today!'

Artificial comments to match her artificial looks, Una thought to herself, a modern day Cruella de Vil if ever there was one.

Tinker paced up and down nervously but kept a safe distance. He looked distinctly nervous and out of place in the orderly school setting, he was probably worrying that Mr Pinchcod might order him to stand in a corner or write out lines.

Mrs Smith, alias Cruella Mark 2 swiftly glossed over Sebastien but allowed her eyes to settle squarely on Una's face and there they stopped like the hands of a rundown clock. Her intimidating eyes scrutinised Una's features so intensely that Una felt distinctly uncomfortable and blushed.

'Una is my top achieving student.' Mr Pinchcod said proudly, breaking the awkward silence. 'I'm sure she will make an excellent learning companion for your daughter.... what did you say her name was?'

'It's Rosie.' Mrs Smith replied with a curt smile.

'Ah yes, Rosie, what a lovely name.' The head purred. 'I 'm beginning to sense already that Rosie and Una will make a very happy learning partnership.'

'Why isn't Rosie with you today to see the school for herself?' Una asked. 'Doesn't she have a say in important matters like her education?' Una didn't believe for one minute the woman even had a child, let alone one called Rosie who might be interested in joining their class. This bogus daughter was merely a smoke-screen to gain them access into the school.

Mr Pinchcod looked slightly unsettled by Una's audacious questioning while Verity, hiding beneath the desk gave Una a sharp pinch on the ankle for chatting unnecessarily with the evil woman who she wanted to pass swiftly on.

'Unfortunately our sweet Rosie was not feeling well this morning, a bit of a cough and a sniffle, otherwise she would certainly have wished to be with us. She is so looking forward to having new friends and a new school.'

'I'm sorry to hear that Mrs Smith, but you are correct not to introduce her germs into the classroom. We are ever alert to the health and safety needs of our pupils.' Mr Pinchcod declared earnestly and quickly wiped his hands against his jacket pockets.

Una used the moment to ask another question about the bogus daughter. 'Perhaps I might call on Rosie at your home to meet her when her cold improves? I may be able to help her prepare for the school's routines.'

'Perhaps you may.' The woman replied dismissively and intended to bring an end to the conversation by moving on, but Una stopped her. 'If you jot down your address I'll call by to meet her.' She suggested and held out a pencil and paper close to the woman's powdered face.

'I'm sure that won't be necessary.' Mrs Smith snapped back, smiling broadly but simultaneously flashing Una a hostile look.

Mr Pinchcod coughed and frowned pointedly at Una, somewhat annoyed by her petulant behaviour.

But Una was undeterred and determined to outwit this devious Cruella lookalike.

'It's nothing. Really. I can call around after school tonight just to introduce myself so your daughter has a friendly face to turn to on her first day. A new school can be such a daunting experience.'

Una felt another, more insistent pinch on her ankle, from Verity and had to stifle a yelp. Verity was getting crosser and crosser while Una appeared to be engaging in unnecessary tittle-tattle and increasing the risk of her being discovered.

But this time Verity was saved by the increasingly agitated Mr Pinchcod who led the woman firmly away before Una could make any more inappropriate suggestions which might further upset the apple cart.

Still Verity was not quite out of the woods yet, for just as the woman was ushered away, Mr Smith, otherwise known as Tinker, took his turn to amble closer.

He hesitated in the library area only momentarily and was about to follow his better half when Una leapt up and deliberately pushed her chair into his path.

'Oh dear, I'm sorry.' She apologised when his shins raked against the wooden rim.

Having successfully halted his escape, Una gave the man a polite smile and asked. 'While you have a moment, sir, could you remind me of your daughter's name? I'd really like to be her friend when she comes for her first day at the school.'

Mr Smith, increasingly out of his depth in the classroom setting hesitated with a slightly befuddled expression furrowing his brow, but then his features brightened like a lightbulb as when a person remembers an essential item on a shopping list.

'Ah yes, It's Ruby.' He said and clicked his fingers. 'Yes, Ruby, that's her name alright.' He repeated the name, this time with more confidence.

'Ah yes, Ruby.' Una repeated and spelled the name out aloud writing the words large in her jotter.

The so called Mr Smith bundled on determined to catch up with Mrs Smith who was standing at the doorway ready to leave having inspected the whole class.

Una winked across the table to Sebastien. 'Got him!' She whispered triumphantly.

Chapter 9

It was impossible to approach the old oak without being spotted by any observer who happened to be stationed on watch in the high Eyrie. That's where Una was crouched, unseen but ready to draw up the rope ladder at a moments notice should the need arise.

Her two friends were up there too, Sebastien armed with a wooden fence post and Verity with a large pot of sticky black paint.

'Anybody we don't like the look of approaches those steps and they'll be getting an almighty headache.' Sebastien declared, although everyone who knew him knew he would never harm a fly.

Verity repeatedly twisted her red hair around in a pencil then released it to spring back into its natural curl.

'Events have taken a nasty turn.' She said. 'We are no longer a team of ghost hunters investigating a haunted house, but a team of crime fighters at war with a band of dangerous criminals.'

Verity had survived her latest ordeal beneath the school desk and now the school day was over had an opportunity to feed back her feelings on the encounter with her friends here in the safety of the Eyrie. She was becoming deeply troubled as recent experiences piled one atop another.

'They locked me in darkness, encased me in a giant egg-case and who knows what fate they intended for me. Now I'm having nightmares every night.'

Una squeezed Her friend's hand.

'Next they're hunting me down like a wild animal, even from the safety of my own classroom.'

'Give me a good, honest ghost any day of the week!' Sebastien declared. 'I always feel safe hunting ghosts. You know where you are with a ghost. All ghosts do is make old pipes rattle, or freeze the hair on the back of your neck, or make blood drip from the walls! All very safe and predictable!'

'But these crooks have no code of conduct, they don't care about other people, especially people like us who threaten to scupper their evil plans!' Verity said.

'The question is, what are we to do about them?' Una asked. 'We know for sure now that they're determined to get Verity, and if they get to her they'll be after us too no doubt.'

Sebastien's eyes widened. 'We must devise a plan to save ourselves!' He said dramatically.

The three fell still in contemplation as only the whisper of a slight breeze and the sound of distant birds calling broke the tense silence.

However the calm didn't last! An insistent barking suddenly interrupted from the base of the tree. It was Nelson.

Una hurriedly lowered herself helter-skelter down the rope burning her palms on the way in her haste to greet her old friend. She threw her arms around his neck and Nelson responded with a fond lick of her face.

They had been apart less than a week but greeted each other like long lost friends. Sebastien and Verity soon arrived to join the party.

This happy reunion seemed at first an innocent one, but then Una noticed Nelson was gripping her skirt with his teeth and pulling insistently as if imploring her to action. 'Faithful Hound Alerts Friend to Owner in Distress!' Verity observed seeing the dog's repeated gestures.

'You think Nelson is trying to tell us something?' Sebastien asked.

Nelson gave another tug this time on Una's blouse sleeve.

'I think you're both right, he wants us to follow him.'

They trouped in a line from the school, three humans tailgating a dog like a posse of prison wardens hot on the scent of an escaped convict.

They followed through the churchyard, down the busy main street and before eventually darting down a maze of unfamiliar side roads. It soon became apparent to Una that Nelson was leading them back to the old house.

The three humans struggled awkwardly over the high wall at the communications box while Nelson bounded effortlessly over the hurdle and immediately disappeared into the jungle beyond.

It seems he had abandoned them.

Una led a way through the tangles of ivy and overgrown rhododendrons. With each turn she feared an ambush from the crooks, so when a sudden crashing of branches from ahead broke the stillness her heart filled with trepidation. Thankfully, it was only Nelson returning, this time to tug with even greater urgency on Una's sleeve.

Nelson led to the rear of the house but then unexpectedly shot off at a tangent across the unkept lawns heading towards the small building set on the perimeter.

The building looked in a similar state of disrepair to the main house. It consisted of a corrugated metal shell with an asbestos slate roof, two rotting wooden windows and a flimsy door at the centre. Only the stone chimney breast at one end broke the symmetry.

Nelson halted panting by the door waiting for the humans to catch up.

Sebastien tested the door handle but it was firmly locked, so he knocked politely on the wood, but no reply came.

'This must be where Nelson's owner lives.' Verity said.

'Mr Markham does have the look of a groundsman or a gardener, but if that's the case then he's not a very good one, judging by the state of the house and the grounds.' Sebastien said noting the poor state of repair the house was in.

'And it would seem he's not at home today.' Verity added.

'Or he's unable to answer the door.' Una suggested.

Verity cupped a hand to the windows but both were cloaked with heavy curtains. There was however a small opening pane at the top of one which was slightly opened on its latch. A length of plain netting hung down the outside.

'It looks like Nelson may have made an escape through that open window to bring help. But it's far too small for any human to squeeze through.' Una said.

Sebastien disagreed. 'If Nelson can wriggle through there, then so can I.' He claimed boldly. Without delay, he hoisted himself onto the window ledge and pushed his hands into the opening. Verity took his ankles firmly while his head and body squirmed through the rectangular opening snake-

like, squeezing his ribs into the gap until only a pair of
flailing legs remained dangling outside.

Verity gave a final shove and the legs followed the body into
the building. A clashing and a clattering of falling pots and
pans suggested Sebastien had fallen into a kitchen area,
which in fact he had.

He picked himself from the floor and wandered cautiously
into what appeared to be someone's cosy living area where
an open fire still smouldered in the grate. A matching pair of
worn armchairs were arranged to each side of the fire and a
small table set between was cluttered with a collection of
old items; a box camera, several engine parts and a framed
photograph of a man with his dog.

Sebastien thought he recognised a younger Mr Markham in
his country wear with Nelson posted by his side.

Above the mantelpiece were several brass horseshoes
mounted on leather straps and in the middle a large
wooden clock which ticked off the seconds.

Damp clothing hung drying before the dying fire on a
wooden clothes-horse and next to that an oak bookcase
bulged with glossy magazines and country life editions.

Then Sebastien saw the body on the rug almost hidden by
the drying clothes. The mouth was tightly gagged with tape
and the hands and legs roughly bound behind his back.
Sebastien had met the man only once before, on the wrong
end of a gun, but he recognised him immediately as Mr
Markham.

At first the body seemed lifeless and Sebastien feared the
worst. He had never witnessed a dead body before,
certainly not the body of a murder victim, and he wasn't

sure what one looked like. He hesitated uncertain of what to do next. If he touched the body his fingerprints might incriminate him in the crime.

Putting aside his fears he decided he must act quickly and took a shoulder to lift the body. It was surprisingly light. But on rolling the man over Sebastien found a pair of bulging wide eyes starring back directly into his own. 'Get me out of this mess!' They pleaded.

Without wasting a second Sebastien ripped away the tape from the thin mouth, an action which caused Mr Markham to let out a blood curdling yell.

'I'm so sorry, I didn't mean to hurt you!' Sebastien apologised raising his arms in alarm. His words were rapidly followed by a frantic banging on the door.

'What's happening, Sebastien? Are you alright in there?' Verity called through the letterbox.

'Untie my festering hands!' Mr Markham demanded now that his tongue was freed.

Sebastien was caught in two minds - should he unlock the door to allow his friends in, or should he undo the knots as Mr Markham demanded?

He chose knots, as the old gent's needs looked more urgent, like he might suffer a heart attack at any moment.

Sebastien recalled seeing a kitchen knife resting on the wooden draining board where he'd climbed in and quickly retrieved it. He soon got to work cutting through the knots using much care to avoid slashing into the old man's skin and after some delicate work with the blade the last knot came undone and the man was able to sit up, badly cramped but free at last.

He barely had time to recover his wits when there came a deafening crash of splitting wood from the hallway and splinters filled the air as the door to the house exploded inwards as if struck by a hand-grenade.

Nelson came bounding through the newly made hole promptly followed by Una and Verity who between them carried the sawn remains of a long length of tree trunk.

'What in suffering socks name do you think you're doing?' Mr Markham cried in amazement.

'We heard a scream and thought Sebastien must be in trouble.' Una explained. 'So we had to do something fast.'

'Therefore the makeshift battering ram.' Verity added and threw the trunk to the floor seeing that its work was done.

Mr Markham soon calmed down. It seemed everyone was safe and now that he had been rescued his mood lightened.

'That may come in handy later for kindling.' He said noting that his fire was almost out. He examined the cuts and bruises on his wrists where the rope had cut into the skin.

'You saved my life, kids!' He said. 'Nobody ever visits me here, I could have lain on the floor for weeks undiscovered, without food or water. I'd have suffered an agonising death.'

'It's Nelson you need to thank, Mr Markham. He's the one who alerted us to the danger.' Una said and she gave Nelson a hug.

'He is a clever lad, and loyal too.' Mr Markham replied. 'He knew I needed help, and what's more he knew exactly where to find it.'

'So those crooks are on to you too, I guess?' Sebastien asked.

'You're right, lad. Yesterday tea, it was. Caught them sniffing around in the grounds. I had every right to threaten them with the police when it's my duty to look after the old place.' Mr Markham gave a painful grimace. 'But there were too many of them, for an old man of my age. Three of the biggest thugs overpowered me, tied me up on the floor of my own home, and left me there to die.'

Mr Markham felt strong enough to stand now. Verity brought him a glass of water. He took a sip, lifted a green raincoat from a hook and draped it over his back then slung the same long barrelled gun he'd aimed at Una over his shoulder.

'What do you intend to do?' Una asked in a whisper.

'I'm going to show those heartless crooks the wrong end of my rifle, that's what I'm going to do!' He replied, and taking no further interest in his guests stepped through the gap where the door had once been and departed with Nelson following closely at his heels.

'Anger is a Poor Master!' verity declared as he strode off towards the house.

'Yes, but revenge is sweet!' Una replied. 'Come on, he's going to need our help.' All three took off after him.

When Mr Markham came to the old house he dispensed with the usual formality of opening the door, instead giving the wood a high kick with his size ten boot followed by two extra hard ones for good effect. And that was the second door to be reduced to firewood in as many minutes.

He marched up the staircase and into the room where the stolen goods were stored and where Verity had been taken hostage only a few days previously.

But now the room was bare and it echoed with a hollow ring. It seems the crooks had departed, done a runner, and taken the loot with them.

'Darn it!' Mr Markham exclaimed. He kicked a chair in frustration then banged his fists on the marble table.

A moment later the fire in his eyes died and he suddenly became aware he was not alone, that a trio of children were watching wide eyed his every move.

'You kids need to get off home. Those crooks are far too dangerous for youngsters to be getting involved with. I'll sniff them out myself and bring them to justice. Wait and see. Come on Nelson.'

He shepherded his faithful companion away and they heard the size ten boots clomping down the staircase before dying away into the distance.

Verity groaned. 'Not a grisly ghost, nor a stolen sausage, not even a crooked crook to be found. Looks like we're back to square one, guys!'

Chapter 10

Una enjoyed her stops by Vincent's book shop, especially at the end of a tiring day in school. The little cramped room was ordinary enough, but the hundreds of books lining the walls were anything but ordinary.

Their pages were filled with tales of adventure, mystery and the daring exploits of amazing people. They thrilled the imagination and Una never ceased to be astonished by the incredible stories which she discovered inside their sleeves. Today she flopped lazily into the leather armchair and breathed out a sigh of relief.

Yet it seemed to Una that no matter what dangers the characters of books came up against in their fictional worlds, the heroes always emerged safely from their adventures, unscathed from the terrifying exploits they faced, the author carefully guiding the reader to a satisfying conclusion, to a happily ever after.

Una mused on, thinking of her own real life experiences of recent weeks. Harsh reality, as it was known, she was beginning to realise, often brought less satisfying conclusions than those of storybooks, or even the destruction of people's hopes and aspirations.

She unfolded the brief note scribbled into her jotter and read the single word. 'Ruby'.

Her heart missed a beat again as she recalled the encounter with the two bogus parents in her classroom. Until yesterday she would have poured scorn on the idea that the filthy hands of crime might weasel their way into her school life and seek to undermine her safety under the very nose of her teachers. But that unlikeliest of possibilities was now become reality.

Soon the nautical belly came steaming down the aisle cup in hand, and swung into the docking bay beside her chair.

'Thank you so much Vincent, I need this to calm my nerves.' Una said and she lifted the cup to her lips to sip the refreshing brew.

'You're welcome my dear, had a frightful week have we?' He asked.

'It's been awful, Vincent.' Una admitted. 'I've had a scrape with the most unpleasant woman in the world, plus her equally unpleasant family of crooks.' She replaced the half emptied cup to its saucer.

'Really? In my schooldays the big problems were always of the mathematical type. For instance, I never could understand why a nautical mile had to be longer than an ordinary mile. It made no sense to me!'

'But more than that I miss having my dog friend to walk.' Una continued with a sigh. 'Nelson was such a faithful companion to have by my side.'

'I know exactly how you feel, Una. Isn't it the truth that dogs never make demands on you, or have unreasonable expectations?'

Una finished her tea.

'I have a challenge for you, Vincent!' She exclaimed.

'Wonderful! I love a challenge, or a voyage of adventure, or a mystery of the deep, anything like that to break the monotony, fire away, Una!'

'I'm afraid it's nothing exciting. I was hoping you might be able to find me a book about life in the alum works at Ravenscar, or something along those lines?'

'Hmm, I do have a whole section on local history, but the alum works at Ravenscar seems to be a very popular subject of late. That ignorant thug who dropped anchor here last week trawled up several of my best titles. But never mind, I have a secret Davy Jones locker which holds many more undiscovered titles!'

The belly reversed around, navigated between the islands of books and sailed away over the horizon.

It must have been a short voyage, for in only a matter of minutes the belly re-emerged, this time loaded with a cargo of books balanced on the bow.

'This should keep you busy.' He said and dropped three books into Una's lap.

Poor Bookworm jumped in surprise at the unexpected delivery which almost flattened her tail. She stretched out a paw in annoyance and shook the coils on her spine, but then realised the storm was over and snuggled back into a sleepy ring.

When the ship's bell sounded only moments later the old cat was already fast asleep. 'Another customer! It's my lucky day!' Vincent exclaimed and the belly set sail again to cruise through the narrow channel.

Una opened the first of the books while Bookworm purred contentedly in her lap. She began to read.

Alum production it seemed was a long process involving numerous stages, intense manual labour and many months of processing before the precious crystals were purely formed and ready to be shipped out to London or the northern industrial towns.

It seems alum crystals acted like magic to fix the dyes in fashionable woollen fabrics, and ensure the colours stayed bright for longer and without fading.

Una's tired eyes soon lost focus and the small print began to blur. The events of a busy day, together with the stuffy warmth of the room and the gentle purring of Bookworm lulled her mind into a dreamy snooze.

It was an unexpected movement, or a sound which shattered her slumber, a grey shadow or a creak of a floorboard, but whatever it was Una was suddenly wide awake and alert. Somebody else was in the room.

She opened an eye hoping to see Vincent there, but no, to her horror she saw it was the bogus parent, Cruella Mark 2 herself, looming over her, inspecting her face intently.

Una froze and cursed herself for being so naive, so stupid, for it now seemed obvious the woman had followed her, tracked her every step from school to bookshop, watching and waiting for her to enter the little private room.

Una blushed red faced with embarrassment and tried to conceal the books with their incriminating titles. But the woman was too quick. She grabbed Una's wrist in a vice-like grip and squeezed the tender flesh with her bony fingers until the flow of blood dried up and her arm screamed out with pain.

The woman's grip was so intense that Una was powerless to escape or break free.

Una was in such panic her brain wouldn't think, or instruct her voice to call for help. So she winced in pain until the salty tears which welled behind her eyelids began to escape at last in smeary tracks down her pale cheeks.

'So you have an interest in the old alum works at Ravenscar?' The woman said, spitting with venom as she read the title of the book in Una's lap. 'How strange! I wonder why the ruins of a long past age should be of interest to a modern young lady such as yourself?'

'Mind your own business!' Una replied through gritted teeth mustering her voice at last. She tried again to break free from the vice-hold but the woman only increased the pressure further and bent Una's arm back until it seemed her poor bone must surely snap in two.

'I don't like you.' The woman sneered into Una's ear through blood red lipstick. 'I don't like your clever attitude, and I don't like your sneaky ways.'

Keeping the lock on her arm tight she reached into Una's satchel and began to rifle through the contents looking for anything of interest or value. Una was powerless to stop her. Mostly Una stored school books and paperwork in the satchel, but the woman's fingers eventually alighted on the little lead soldier which Edward had given her. She examined it with some curiosity, then deciding it may have value, transferred the toy into her own pocket.

'If I were you, I'd stay well clear of those alum works in future. You may be safe in school while your friends are close by, or here in the town where many people are about, but if I were to catch you alone, out on those remote cliff tops, you never know what might happen to you. People have nasty accidents on cliffs. They wander too close to the edge, they accidentally fall off, they disappear into the sea at night when no-one's watching and drown, far from the help of their loved ones.'

The woman's red lips cooed so near to Una's cheek she felt the damp warmth of her breath press on her skin.

Fortunately for Una, the evil woman's threats were brought to a sudden halt by a pair of grizzled faces which poked around from the bookshelves, not friendly faces, but the weasely ones of Ferrit and Richter.

'Tinker says we have to leave right away, Amphety.' Ferrit told the woman. 'The old bookshop owner is having palpitations for some reason. He might not last much longer before he has a heart attack!'

The woman reluctantly eased her grip and threw Una's wrist to the table. Then as a parting gift she slapped Una across the cheek with an open palm.

Before she left she turned to point a bony finger at Una. 'Remember, stay clear of the cliffs for your own safety, darling.' She warned, then followed Ferrit and Richter down the long aisle of books. A moment later Una heard the ship's bell signal their exit from the shop.

Even before she had time to compose herself, Vincent came thundering into the room looking pale and distressed.

'Una, thank goodness you're safe.' He gasped. 'I've never been so frightened in my whole life. Two of those dreadful thugs have had me pinned up against the till while their accomplices ransacked the safe, no doubt intent on stealing my whole life's savings.'

The bookshop owner took a deep breath to steady himself, thought briefly, then added. 'Not that I have any life savings to steal. But if I did have any life savings they'd be gone!'

'I'm fine, Vincent, don't worry about me. I kept out of their way. That woman struck me as an unpleasant piece of work the moment she walked into the room.' Una didn't want to burden Vincent with the ugly truth.

Vincent wiped his brow with a velvet shelf duster.

'Thankfully I banked everything yesterday and the whole gang have left empty handed. Serves them right, frightening innocent law abiding folk like us.' The distraught shopkeeper took another lungful of air then added.

'Make me a cup of tea, Una, I feel all weak in the bilges.'

Chapter 11

'It was like one of those bad nightmares, you know, the type where you want to escape but you can't because your body is glued to the spot.' Una said. Verity examined the purple bruises and red fingernail indents on her wrist.

Una winced, more in memory of the event rather than pain. 'At least I found out her name. 'Amphety,' one of them called her as he left.'

'Amphety, what sort of name is that?' Verity asked.

The Eyrie rocked gently on the breeze and gave a tranquility quite at odds with the mood of its occupants. Una's encounter with the Amphety woman had left her shocked and unsettled.

'First they kidnap Verity, then they attack Mr Markham and leave him for dead, and now you Una, attacked and intimidated in broad daylight.' Sebastien said. 'I guess I must be next!' He added gloomily.

'I'd like to know where they are now and what their next move is going to be' Verity said. 'If we knew the answer to that we could plan an attack of our own and retaliate first!'

'I bet they've packed the stolen property into the back of the white van and driven the lot down to the coast by now. All ready to be shipped abroad.' Sebastien replied.

'And if we don't get our act together the whole caboodle will dissolve like smoke into the criminal mists of Europe!' Verity complained.

Una felt sure the crooks intended to smuggle the goods from the coast although she couldn't work out how the crooks intended to get the heavy load down the cliffs to the sea.

'Our only clue is the alum works near Ravenscar. I don't know what, but there's definitely something dodgy going on there. Why else would they kidnap Verity and lock her up in one of those strange insect pods? We should stake the place out, see if the crooks put in an appearance.'

'That's a good plan Una, but we'll need transport.' Sebastien observed.

'A Top Job for Super Cleaner?' Verity asked. They all nodded approval and promptly made an escape down the rope to seek out Aggie.

They found her tinkering about under the hood of her jeep, it being a weekend.

'We're pretty sure the crooks plan to smuggle their stolen goods out of the country, so the coast is the most likely place for us to catch them in the act.' Una told Aggie as the caretaker tightened a spark plug.

'And we desperately want to thwart their evil plans!' Verity declared, still smarting from being kidnapped.

'Then we need to get mobile fast!' Aggie replied and she jerked down the bonnet to the engine compartment. 'Jump aboard crime fighters!'

They raced through the town passing Mr Pinchcod as he enjoyed a relaxing stroll on his rest day. The grumpy headmaster frowned with annoyance at the sight of his caretaker racing down the road at breakneck speed with pupils from his own school hanging from the windows. He made a note to interrogate her when the next opportunity arose. Certain safeguarding issues needed to be urgently resolved.

Before the hour was out the old jeep came bumping down the track to the now familiar ruins of the old alum works. Aggie switched off the noisy engine and they sat in silence, watching, waiting, hoping to catch a sign of suspicious criminal activity.

More time passed, nothing happened. The sea just kept coming in and out and the wind rattled the flags over the little information kiosk. Little had changed since their last visit except that the damaged shutter to the window where the insect eggs were stored had been repaired.

Monotony set in. The seats in the jeep were cramped and uncomfortable. Una began to believe their suspicions about the crooks were unfounded or that they had taken fright and made alternative plans. Poor Aggie, she thought, made to drive all the way to the coast on her rest day and all for nothing.

Aggie yawned and stretched out her fat arms so that everybody had to duck to avoid being seriously injured by the flying ham.

'I really do need my afternoon beauty kip.' She declared at last. 'Do you lot mind if I flake out in the back? It is my rest day, after all.'

They took the hint and climbed out through an opened window while Aggie crawled into the back and zipped up the canvas screen for privacy.

Sebastien wanted to get some photographs of adders sunbathing on the rocks and despite her reluctance led

Verity to a clump of ferns with her tablet at the ready to snap a shot or two.

Una strode out across the coastal path intending to use the spare time more productively. She carried one of Vincent's books about the alum works under one arm and eventually found a secluded seat of rock where she might read awhile in solitude.

Guided by the illustrations in the book she was able to map out the position of the original alum buildings despite the fact that only a few jagged foundations survived.

She picked out two humps like giant mole hills, which she decided must be a pair of clamps, the artificial hills made by buried shale rock.

Then she recognised the squat foundations of a processing block where the alum crystals would have been extracted from the rocks, and beyond that the engine shed and a blacksmith's shop. In the distance towards the cliff edge were the low remains of a row of workers' cottages.

Una visualised the entire community spread out before her, the scene being so vividly etched on her imagination. She could almost hear the noise of industry and the bustle of workers. So when Edward arrived and sat next to her she hardly noticed.

'I have to go back in time to find out about the two ghost children.' He stated at last to draw her attention. 'I need to find out why they haunt the cliffs and what makes them so unhappy.'

Una sat up. 'What dreadful event must have occurred to lock two ghost children in such a lonely place for centuries on end?' She asked.

She scanned the horizon where a darker blue line marked the point where blue sea met blue sky.

'I find it so incredible that you are able to travel in time with such ease Edward, here one moment, gone the next, like a will o' the wisp!'

'I'm still trying to understand it myself. I used to think that time only existed in the present moment, you know, like a spark, and the past was dead while the future yet to happen.'

'But more recently I've been wondering if time might be more like a vast tunnel winding through space with everybody alive and existing on their own life journey at different parts of the time tunnel.'

'It seems like I've accidentally discovered a way to escape the fabric of the tunnel which enables me to jump from one point in the tunnel and re-join it at another.'

'You think you may have discovered a way of travelling between the past and the future through a space tunnel?' Una asked, unlikely as the idea sounded to her.

'That's my best explanation I have of what's happening to me.' Edward agreed.

Una found the idea fascinating but had to pull herself back to reality. 'That Edward, is the most interesting conversation about tunnels I have ever had. And in normal circumstances I'd be riveted. But at this particular moment in time I'm on an urgent mission to catch a gang of dangerous crooks and l mustn't be distracted by your mad, fantastical theories!'

Edward threw up his arms in frustration. 'That's the whole problem with people like you, Una! You're all so tied up in your own little problems that you fail to see the bigger picture!'

Edward was right in a sense, Una's mind was indeed full of her own problems, but hers were real problems, they urgently needed attention, unlike Edward's theoretical ideas about space tunnels, which might defy solution forever for all Una knew.

Their debate may have delved further into Edward's thoughts about time travel, but their conversation was interrupted by a sudden commotion further along the cliff. A skid of wheels, a harsh squeal of brakes, the slam of heavy doors and the sound of gruff voices raised in anger.

It came from the vicinity of a white van which had been driven at speed down the track before swinging perilously over the uneven ground and slamming to an emergency stop near the brick shed.

Una watched from a distance as two men leapt from between the doors and immediately took up chase of two fleeing children. These were Verity and Sebastien scrambling like rabbits over the rough terrain as they made their desperate bid to escape capture.

The men were hunting down them down like trained hunting dogs, twisting, turning, snapping and snarling. Una crossed her fingers hoping her youthful friends might escape, but it was not to be, there was nowhere to flee, no bolt hole to take safe refuge.

She watched on helplessly as the white van's engine burst back into life, the wheels churned and accelerated then swerved into the path of her two friends intending to cut them off, or mow them down.

Ferrit captured Verity first and hoisted her over his back with as much care as a sack of potatoes. She beat him on the back with her fists but to no avail.

Sebastien came next. He turned his head to see Verity being captured then turned back intending to rescue her, only to be easily overpowered by the two heavies and Richter. There was a brief scuffle before both he and Verity were thrown roughly into the back of the van and the two white doors slammed shut behind them.

Una flattened herself into the shadows fearing she too should suffer a similar fate. But Ferrit and Richter were more interested in the parked jeep. Una expected the men to reach inside and drag out the grumpy Aunt Aggie from her afternoon snooze on the rear seat.

Instead, Richter leaned his body through the driver's side window and released the handbrake while Ferrit pushed a hefty shoulder up against the bumper.

With a sudden creak the wheels began to roll forward, slowly at first, but gradually gathering pace until quite rapidly the whole vehicle began to pitch forward down the slope with its nose tossing up and down out of control.

Una leapt up in alarm, careless now of being spotted.

'Hey! Auntie Aggie's asleep in the back, she'll get injured!' She cried, and sprinted full pelt towards the runaway vehicle.

But Una was much too far away to be heard and in any case the wind carried her voice in the opposite direction.

The jeep careered relentlessly towards the cliff edge gathering speed with every passing second. Time and again the whole caboodle seemed destined to somersault onto its roof and be smashed to smithereens, yet by some miracle each time it managed to right itself again.

Una covered her mouth in horror as she realised the inevitable disaster that was about to unfold before her very wide eyes. The end of Aggie and her precious jeep had turned into a certainty.

With a final contorted leap the vehicle catapulted into the air and launched over the cliff edge like a rocket into space. But the jeep was not a rocket, it was aerodynamically unfit and the momentum was soon lost. The bonnet took a sudden nose-dive and returned earthwards plummeting like a boulder.

Una raced to the brim to see Aggie's pride and joy plunge downwards, crashing in a series of metal tearing rolls and crunching collisions, smashing again and again against the rock face until it crashed at last into the sea far below with an enormous sploosh and an explosion of steam.

The wreckage settled in half a metre of water and lay there a moment until a huge wave topped the canvas roof and swept the wreckage underneath.

Una felt herself lightheaded and her eyes blurred with hot tears.

'Aggie was sleeping in the car!' She screamed. 'You've murdered her!'

Chapter 12

Edward travelled through a land of grey smoke and thunder. The same one Una inhabited, only the two friends did not cross paths, for the alum works Edward walked existed two hundred years before that of Una's. The buildings Edward walked through were not ancient foundations but those of a fully working factory, alive with people.

Men in dungarees, bodies silhouetted against the grey-white cliff, toiled with pick and spade like so many busy insects. Noise and fire burnt everywhere. Edward's lungs filled with a bitter taste of acrid fumes which poured from chimneys and doorways all around. Black smoke curled lazily from a mountain of smouldering rock. Workmen shepherded a stream of bubbling liquid along a shallow trough before it diverted into a nearby red brick building. Everywhere was a hub of activity.

Edward came at length to a row of pretty, yet simple cottages. This must be the place where the two children lived, but all was serene and Edward found no trace of any recent tragedy.

The dreadful event had not yet taken place.

Close by the cottages a scattering of women bent to gather vegetables into woven baskets, they walked up and down the strip of lush green land their simple clothing contrasting sharply against the distant blue of the sea.

Edward stopped to watch them at work and became absorbed in their repetitive movements until his thoughts were rudely interrupted by a chuckle in his ear.

'Are you sleeping?' A voice asked. It was a little girl. She and her brother had sneaked up from behind as he watched the women at their work.

Edward examined the two children closely and wondered if they were the ones he had been summoned to help.

'You must be new here, we haven't seen you before.' The girl observed seeing he was awake now.

'I am indeed new.' Edward replied. He wanted to tell her he was a traveller in time but decided not to complicate the issue just yet. 'I'm only passing through.'

This statement caused a huge deal of merriment, and the two children laughed aloud.

'Passing through to where?' The boy asked.

Edward peered along the coast, but there was nothing of note other than heather as far as the eye could see. Then he remembered the name of the town Una had mentioned.

'Robin Hood's Bay.' He said. The girl and boy eyed each other with mischievous smiles and laughed aloud again.

'We've never been anywhere.' The boy stated glumly his mood changing as quick as lightning.

'We were born here, in that house over there.' The girl added and she nodded her head in the direction of the middle cottage.

'So you know this place like the back of your hands, I guess?' Edward asked.

Both children examined the back of their hands studiously then laughed out loud again and rolled back into the grass.

'If you want, we can give you a tour.' The girl suggested once she had regained her composure.

'I'd like that.' Edward replied.

The girl took a hand and the boy the other and they set off up the slope towards the quarry face.

Soon they came to a long, low brick building with a pan-tiled roof dotted all along with opening windows where smoke and steam escaped into the air.

'These are the alum buildings.' The girl explained, sounding like an expert despite her age. Edward sneaked a look inside through an opened door. Rows of baths were being filled with steaming liquid.

'We boil the alum liquid in the baths then leave it to cool. That way the dirty bits settle to the bottom so we can get rid of them.'

'Daddy says we must make the alum pure and crystal clear.' The boy added.

'What do you use the alum for?' Edward asked looking along the rows of emerald green pans. The question brought renewed peels of laughter from his companions.

'We don't know that!' They said in unison.

'We only make the crystals, then they get taken away on boats to the big towns and cities.'

'Who knows what happens to them there?' The boy remarked.

'Those magic crystals are used to make clothes look pretty.' The girl said showing off her superior knowledge.

Urging him on Edward followed the building's wall until a second door allowed another glimpse inside.

Here sweaty workers poured tubs of scalding water over the crystals while others dismantled wooden shuttering from a large cylindrical cask.

'Those are the solid blocks of pure alum.' The girl told Edward proudly.

'They're so heavy it's impossible to lift one.' The boy told him.

'So the block has to be ground down into a powder and bagged. Then it's ready to be loaded onto the railway.'

'The railway?' Edward echoed, reminded suddenly of his own life pulling tram horses.

The children again burst into peels of gleeful laughter. 'Don't you know anything?' They asked.

'This is the winding house we're at now.' The boy explained as they approached a new brick building. A railway track led out from the doors and across to the steep cliff edge directly above the beach. Edward looked over the drop and imagined the heavily laden carriage being lowered down the cliff to the base where men waited to load the crystals safely onto a boat.

The day was growing late now and darkness already crept over the smoky buildings. An alarm sounded bringing groups of workers from the cliff face after their day's shift. Yellow Lamps began to blink on in the alum buildings and cottages.

'We have to go now.' The boy said.

'We have our lessons.' The girl explained.

Edward cast his eye over the buildings. 'Where is the school?' He asked.

The girl laughed. 'There is no school, silly! Our mother teaches us at home.'

'She's very strict!' The boy complained.

Left alone now, Edward escaped a distance from the noise and the glow of the fires and sat alone in the sweet smelling heather.

Time travel, he decided, was a lonely occupation. A boy was always distant from his friends, not only in kilometres, but in time too.

He wondered if Una was safe. If it be known, she was only a few metres from where he himself sat, but two hundred years into the future. He lay back his head and mused as the evening drew on.

Then a sudden break in the clouds revealed a sky full of stars and an owl screeched in the distance reminding Edward of his friend, Sebastien. How he would love to be here in the darkness listening to the calls of the wild creatures.

Bathed in such thoughts Edward soon slept.

He awoke with a start. Darkness and the unfamiliar ground confused his mind. It was night, yes, but in which century he could not say. Was he in the old stables by the Victorian tramline, or in the churchyard where he and Una met, or on the remote clifftops of Ravenscar?

Nor could he say with any certainty what had caused him to awake with such a start. Was it a sound or an instinctive response to danger?

Whichever, when he scanned his eyes across the scene nothing appeared amiss. Fires glowed, a soft hum of distant machinery buzzed the air, blurry yellow lights scattered the darkness from a handful of doorways. Yes, he decided at last, he was at the alum works on the high coast and all seemed at peace.

Yet, something had disturbed his sleep, had set him uneasy.
It was the two children, the ones he had come to save!
He knew they were in peril, but danger lurked all around, in
the great burning fires, in the poisonous gases that clung in
the air, in burning liquids and in the vast moving parts of
colossal machinery.

'How am I to know which deadly hazard is to be
responsible for their deaths when so many dangers lurk all
around?' Edward asked himself.

Irritated by his inability to solve the problem he followed a
dim track back to the buildings and there at last he found
his answer.

Of all the ever present dangers it was the most innocent
little handle that did the damage.

The metal lever of a handbrake, a lever which on a thousand
previous occasions had held firm the heavy wheels, locked
them tightly stopped, but on this one instance had failed,
allowed the massive wheels to squeeze free and then begin
to slowly rotate until at last the heavy wagon had gathered
speed and momentum and in no time was careering
driverless and out of control down the track.

With two children hidden inside!

Edward had watched them climb the steep sides and drop
inside. Perhaps they were playing a game of hide and seek,
or using the steep sided wagon to shelter from the cold
wind.

Whatever their intentions, their tiny movements had
triggered that final straw which caused those heartless
brakes to fail.

Edward saw the danger but too late. Still he jumped into action his legs racing after the truck as it gathered pace. His heart pounded as he stumbled over the uneven ground almost falling more than once. But he somehow managed to keep his balance until he took a huge desperate leap into the darkness.

His nimble fingers latched firmly to the metal sides. A fraction of a second more and the wagon would have passed beyond his reach resulting in a deadly fall beneath the huge iron wheels.

The children had cowered in a corner, frightened by the sudden speed and thundering noise, clutching to the frame, shocked and too traumatised to move. The mighty wheels rattled down the track towards the cliff edge.

Edward clung on. He called out a warning to men at their night posts and they in turn shouted the alarm to men further down the track in the steeping pits and so on, setting off a hue and cry.

Several men who worked closer to the track leapt out attempting to halt the wagon's headlong rush, fearful for the two innocent children clinging on inside, but all to no avail.

Edward stood aloft now, both arms raised in warning, shouting til his lungs might burst.

'Help! Out of control! Children on board.' He repeated over and again.

Next the wagon raced passed the tall walls and chimneys of the alum works itself. More sweat drenched workers dashed out drawn by the hullabaloo, but still the wagon rushed on past.

Edward was dizzy with fear. He half wished he might be whisked away from the danger and returned to his own time, to leave the children to their own fates.

But no, he could not leave them. So he clung on though it seemed his knuckles must break, and the runaway wagon sped on til he knew it must surely break free from the track to smash headlong into the row of cottages.

Finally the alarm reached the ears of a gang of railway workers who toiled late into the night repairing part of the track, and this proved to be fortunate.

These men were better prepared for an emergency and one of them, an athletic youth, sprinted alongside the carriage holding his cap in hand. When the opportunity arose he leapt bravely onto the side and clung on when all others would have failed. He reached out to a long handle, attached to the same brake mechanism which had in the first instance caused the whole drama.

The wagon travelled at breakneck speed now and the metal wheels glowed white with heat, but nevertheless the athletic youth leant his body against the handle using his cap as a pad and forced the brake pads to engage with the wheels buying the occupants a few extra valuable seconds.

Looking ahead Edward saw the track coming to an abrupt end on the brow of the cliff only metres away. At this point the metal rails which had so far guided the wagon safely on its journey suddenly ceased.

Edward realised swift action was called for, otherwise the wagon would be dashed over the edge and they would all perish in the fall, or be drowned in the sea far below.

With moments to spare, he grabbed the two infants firmly by the scruff of their necks as he would a pair of newborn kittens. Then calling to warn the youth that he too must bail out, took another leap into the darkness.

A second later the huge wagon gave an ear splitting thud, skidded off the rails and shot like a missile over the cliff. Then after all the deafening noise there came a strange silence.

Edward was alive, and the two children lay in the heather by his side crying for their mother. They had been catapulted into a thick bed of mossy weeds which had miraculously cushioned their fall.

Close by the athletic youth brushed himself down nonchalantly and replaced the cap to his head.

The gang of engine men rushed up closely followed by a crowd of workers, and lastly the parents of the children themselves who were frantic with worry. They grabbed the infants around the chest and hugged each one tightly with their faces smeared in tears of relief.

Edward checked himself for broken bones and found nothing more serious than a few cuts and bruises.

By this time the workers had formed a close circle around Edward and the athletic youth, every one of them eager to offer thanks and congratulations for their bravery.

'You are a hero young man!' One exclaimed and shook Edward's hand energetically. 'What courage!' Another proclaimed and slapped him heartily on the back.

Soon, when it became clear that Edward, the athletic youth and the two children were unscathed and safe from their perilous ordeal the workers began to wander back to their places of work or their homes to tell their friends and relations of the night's drama.

Edward was left alone in the darkness.

As he wondered what his next move should be, the chimneys crumbled to dust and the walls of the alum works gradually eroded away into powder until only weeds, clinging ivy and the mossy foundations of walls remained. And then Edward himself was gone.

Chapter 13

Una sat on the bank watching the waves sweeping in and out over the wreck of Aggie's jeep. A forlorn hope persisted inside her mind that Auntie Aggie might suddenly climb unscathed from the mangled remains, but the hope was fantasy of course, for to survive a fall from such a terrible height would require nothing less than a miracle.

Nor had Edward the means to save her. Despite his time travel skills he had no extraordinary powers, no magical potion that might help him restrain a criminal or prevent a jeep from crashing over a cliff face. No, he was not in any sense superhuman.

Even so it did make Una cross when Edward was so elusive, always disappearing at the most critical moment, usually without any consideration for anyone else. Or so it seemed to her.

But then again, she argued, she too must not be blameless, idling away the time here above the waves and listlessly watching the spray break over Aggie's jeep when she knew Sebastien and Verity must be in the most dreadful danger.

So at length she forced herself into action, shrugged off her lethargy and crept between the tall patches of heather until she came at last to the foundations of the old alum buildings. From this vantage point she might watch the crooks unseen.

They were gathered by the door of the white van engaged in a heated debate. Eavesdropping their conversation Una soon gathered that several of the men wanted to drive their

captives to a remote location and dump them in a lay-by.
They hoped the children might not be discovered for some
hours, or even days so the crooks would have time to
complete their plans unhindered.

Tinker and Amphety disagreed claiming that to release the
children might threaten their plans. What's more, they
intended a far more gruesome ending for Una's friends.
In the end the matter was settled in Tinker's favour. Ferrit
and Richter climbed into the back of the white van and
emerged moments later carrying Sebastien and Verity
between them, both were roped and gagged. They bundled
the pair into the little building where Una well knew the
strange insect eggs were stored.

She stole closer. Her black skirt and white blouse blended
into the shadows and made an ideal camouflage.

She didn't need to wait long before Tinker, Richter and the
two heavies made a dash to the van. The engine struck up,
wheels skidded into motion and the white van bounced
away down the track. Una wondered what emergency had
rushed them away with such urgency.

Whatever it was, the new situation favoured her. She
calculated only two crooks now remained inside the
building, still not great odds for sure, but in all probability
Una's best opportunity to mount a rescue. If nothing else
she held the element of surprise.

So she crept slowly forward until after much shuffling came
at last to be crouched directly below the window. By a piece
of good fortune she found a curled jag in the metal shutter
where it had been badly repaired which allowed her a

keyhole view into the inside, enough for her to observe any going-ons.

Squinting through she made out the shape of Sebastien wedged tightly against the wall, a graze above his swollen eye, no doubt the consequence of his brawl with the heavies.

Then a movement drew her attention to a second wall where Ferrit and Amphety were on the point of lowering Verity into one of the insect pods.

Poor Verity, this was her second ordeal of being bundled into a cramped pod. Her arms were tied and tape sealed her mouth. Una could hardly restrain herself from rushing inside to confront the crooks, 'let my friend alone, you horrible beasts,' she wanted to demand, but to do so she knew would only result in her own capture and she must at all costs remain at large.

She heard Ferrit's voice. 'So you managed to escape our clutches last time young lady, but this time we're going to be extra careful to keep you safe. There'll be no avoiding the big drop this time.' Una watched him lower Verity into the pod.

'Our little haul of treasures will be taking a sea journey this evening - over to the continent, and you and your friend will be joining them.' Amphety crooned.

Verity made a series of irate grunts through her nostrils.

'No, you don't need to worry your little head about drowning.' Ferrit assured her. 'Once the two parts are clipped together they are quite watertight.'

'But the pod will make a delightful splash when we launch it from the top of the cliff!' Amphety assured her.

'Apparently these aerodynamic pods can reach speeds of up to 100 kilometres as they plummet off the cliff before splashing down in the sea!'

'Rather like a spaceship returning to Earth, but without the parachute to slow the descent!' Amphety crooned and she and Ferrit both laughed heartily at their cruel humour.

Next it was Sebastien's turn. The pair lowered him inside a pod, packed any spaces with valuables and dropped the lid. A clip snapped securely into place to seal the two halves together and the job was done.

All this time Una was watching with horror from the spy-hole while listening for any warning of the van's return, but all was quiet.

She returned her eye to the spy-hole. Ferrit and Amphety had turned their attention to filling the remaining pods with stolen valuables. Una recognised many of the treasures which had been stored in the old abandoned house; jewellery, precious stones and pearl necklaces among them. She had to duck quickly out of sight when Ferrit began to drag the pods through the doorway to line them up in a row outside. Next he brought out a wagon which fitted neatly onto the metal railway tracks beyond the door.

Now they lifted each pod to sit neatly inside the wagon's frame. Finally Ferrit chained the shells together to form a train of pods inside the wagon.

'I know what they intend to do!' Una suddenly gasped from her hiding place. 'They mean to throw the pods over the cliff so they can be fished out of the sea later and loaded onto a waiting boat just like the alum workers did hundreds of years ago!'

Una recalled how incredibly steep the path to the beach was, far too dangerous to cart down alum powder by hand, so the workers had devised a method of lowering the heavy bags over the cliff on a railway system.

'That's so awful!' Una exclaimed under her breath. 'I can't imagine anything more terrifying than to plummet down the face of a cliff inside a flimsy plastic pod.'

'Then perhaps you'd like to join your friends inside one?' A voice rasped from behind her. 'Then you can find out for yourself what it's like rather than simply imagining it.'

Una jumped out of her skin. It was Tinker. He had sneaked up behind her. Not for the first time she kicked herself for being so naive. It was so obvious. The thugs had driven off as a decoy, to drop Tinker out just beyond sight knowing full well that Una would most likely come looking for her friends as soon as the van had gone.

'You think you're so clever sneaking up on us like that, but I've been watching you all the time.' He gloated.

Tinker grabbed her by the arm and forced her inside where Ferrit and Amphety were clearing up the last of the stolen property into the pods.

'I found her eavesdropping outside the door.' Tinker told them. 'She was chattering away to herself about falling off cliffs, so I thought perhaps she'd like to have a go for herself. Nothing like first hand experience is there, eh?'

They soon had her tied up and her mouth taped.

'You've done enough talking for one day.' Tinker told her as he dumped the poor girl unceremoniously into a remaining pod. Amphety filled any remaining space with stolen

jewellery then snapped the pod closed to engulf Una in
darkness.

'Personally I'd love to know what it's like to ride the scariest
fairground attraction in the world, but truth is I'm too
beautiful to die!' Amphety leered through her red lips.

Una felt herself being carried outside, lifted onto the wagon
and added to the string of pods. Three pods of kids and
three of stolen valuables.

Tinker fastened Una's pod to the rest with a chain.

'We don't want one of you getting lost when you're down
there bobbing up and down on the ocean!' He laughed.

'They're all accounted for now boss, three kids locked safely
in the pods and one pensioner swimming with the fishes in
a wrecked jeep.' Ferrit confirmed.

'We need to get these beauties ready for launching so we
can make our way down to the beach, it'll be dark soon and
our friends on the boat will be waiting to get the cargo
loaded on board.'

Tinker released a brake handle and the wagon began to roll
down the incline towards the cliff edge. As it came to the
brink he cranked the handbrake back on again and the
whole load halted on the cliff edge.

'As soon as the boat's in place we'll send you the signal to
release the brake and send the pods tumbling over the edge
into the sea.' Tinker told Ferrit. Ferrit gave a thumbs up and
positioned himself next to the wagon ready to release the
lever.

'Until then the rest of us need to make our way down to the
beach ready to help load the boat. Come, it's a long haul

down the path.' Tinker ordered and the crooks set off at a brisk pace leaving Ferrit at his station by the pods.

Chapter 14

Aggie ambled out of the rustic clifftop kiosk unwrapping a second choc ice and set out along the coastal path. She loved sweet treats and could never resist anything with a chocolate coating.

But times were tight and on her meagre wages she didn't have enough cash to buy treats for all the kids, so she had sneaked out through the back door of her jeep and legged it across to the little kiosk where a row of flags waving in the wind had attracted her attention.

She stopped at a rickety old bench which looked out across the vast expanse of sea to spend a moment enjoying the feast in peace and quiet then promptly nodded off, as she so often did in recent years due to her advancing years.

When she awoke some time later the remains of her choc ice had melted into a sticky glue on the bench with numerous sugar loving insects tucking in for free.

The sweet taste of the chocolate still lingered on her tongue, and as she was so enjoying the unexpected trip to the seaside she decided to hang the expense and shell out on the cost of a second.

However, the full enjoyment of this double choc-fest became tarnished somewhat when Aggie cast her eyes towards the alum works and quite failed to distinguish the familiar shape of her beloved jeep. Nope, it was not to be seen anywhere near the place where she felt certain she had parked it.

Now a number of quite rational explanations for its absence sprang readily to mind, like for example, she was looking in completely the wrong direction. This sometimes occurred when she parked up in a large supermarket carpark, although on such occasions the confusion arose from there being so very many vehicles all cramped into one small place, whereas in this instance there were no vehicles to be seen for miles.

Or, and this seemed a more plausible explanation, it could be that those pesky kids had nicked her precious jeep while she was in the kiosk buying the choc ices.

Yes, those kids were usually a perfectly sensible lot, she knew, but kids were kids and they were only trustworthy for as long as you could pin your eyes on them. Look away a second and kids immediately turned into raving kleptomaniacs. So she wouldn't put it past them to twok her pride and joy while she was absent.

She decided to investigate further and made her way in the rough direction of where she expected the jeep to be, her mind still racing with all sorts of possibilities. It even crossed her mind that by some inexplicable oversight she had missed a 'No Parking' sign by the track, and that her beautiful green goddess had been towed away by some over zealous traffic warden.

She began to regret her uncontrollable weakness for choc ice as she calculated the ridiculously large fine she might have to pay to get her jeep released from one of those annoying safe compounds.

So taken was she with thoughts of what might be that a badly placed tree root growing on the track took away her ankle and sent the poor caretaker sprawling head over heels into a muddy puddle.

Aggie cursed all town planners and architects and anyone else whose lack of consideration resulted in bloody knees. She hobbled onwards with fresh blood dripping down her shins and her mind wavering between utter wrath and fuzzy headed confusion.

If anyone had damaged her precious jeep they would be in for the high jump, that was for certain and she growled angrily between false teeth.

Yet upon reaching the spot where she felt the trusty vehicle ought to be her old eyes saw nothing apart from a rather unusual set of white pods hanging on a wagon close by the cliff edge. She felt certain the distinctive white pods hadn't been there when she sneaked off for the choc ice.

With no other plan at hand, and not a single kid in sight, she decided to check out the odd looking pills.

'I've a funny feeling they may just have something to do with those pesky kids - and my missing jeep.' She reasoned with herself.

So Aggie made her way down to the edge stepping cautiously to avoid another fall while all the time half expecting a kid to jump out at her from one of the many hidden crevices laughing at her befuddlement. Wouldn't it be just like them to play hide and seek with her, the cheeky little monkeys!

But she took some comfort from the sure knowledge that the last laugh would be hers, for she held possession of the all important car keys for the ride back home.

Then she remembered with a jolt that the jeep had gone so the keys were useless and she scowled again, a dark mood suddenly kindled and all ready to explode into flames!

She picked her way through the undergrowth keeping an eye out for snakes and any rodents who might be attracted to the smell of fresh blood on her knees.

To her utter astonishment when she came to the pods Aggie found not kids but a fully grown man, unshaven and half asleep laid beside the wagon of pods awaiting the signal. It was Ferrit, of course.

She gave him a prod with her toe. The man jumped up startled and gave a cry of shock as he recognised who she was.

'It's you, the woman in the jeep! How on earth did you survive that fall?' He asked in utter disbelief.

Agnes raised her skirt and bent to examine her bloodied knees. While she agreed that a fall at her age wasn't to be recommended, she hardly felt it merited such a shocked response.

'It makes no odds.' Ferrit continued regaining his composure. 'You won't be so lucky this time!' And he grabbed Aggie by the lapels intending to throw her over the edge where she would be instantly reunited with her jeep. But Ferrit had badly misjudged the strength of the wily old caretaker whose ample frame had often been compared to that of a grizzly bear. She took hold of Ferrit's own shoulders and in a flash slam dunked him heavily to the ground. The unfortunate man's head cracked against unforgiving rock and for a brief moment he lost

144

consciousness and the little space behind his eyeballs turned a deep purple.

When he returned to his senses a moment later it was to see the immense outline of the woman with her skirt tied above her knees and her huge torso looming large over him.

Ferrit had always wondered what it would be like to be flattened by a sumo wrestler and now he was about to find out at first hand. For a second Aggie's shadow obliterated the sun like a solar eclipse then she launched herself into the air. The immense body came crashing down on the hapless man cracking several ribs and forcing every drip of air from his crushed lungs.

Aggie climbed off and gave her hands a slap. Nobody messed with her on a bad day!

For a full minute Ferrit was unable to draw breath. His mouth gagged for air and his lips turned a deathly shade of blue. Then drawing on all his reserves of strength, and before another more deadly attack was launched, the broken man half slithered, half crawled to safety. Once a safe distance had been made between himself and the sumo-woman he regained his feet and began to run as fast as his legs would allow, in an opposite direction, all the time clutching his aching ribs.

Ferrit had lost all interest in money, in wealth and in the simple pleasures of crime, all he wanted was to escape, to put distance between himself and the terrifying woman. Yes, he argued to himself, I can live with being poor and penniless, and much rather that than the pain of punctured lungs and broken ribs.

But more than that escape was now Ferrit's only option, for the embarrassment of being smacked down by a woman meant he could never again face Tinker or the gang without feeling utter humiliation.

So he legged it back to the road and as far away as possible. And he never came back.

Aggie rubbed her poor knees then turned her attention to the white pods, which seen close up were much larger than she had first imagined.

She kicked one experimentally with her big toe and found it gave a dull thud. Not hollow she surmised.

'Now, I wonder how these came to be here?' She asked herself aloud. 'Maybe they've got something valuable hidden inside?'

She found the wagon's brake handle on one side and not knowing what it might be gave an experimental tug. Fortunately she resisted the temptation to give a good yank when it dawned on her that doing so might well cause unwanted consequences.

'I think I'll just open one up and take a peek inside.' She said curious now to find what secrets lay within.

She unsnapped a metal spring on the nearest one and gingerly prised the two shells apart.

When the egg cracked apart she could hardly believe her eyes for there cramped inside was none other than Una! 'What in Mrs Beaton's name are you doing in there?' She asked in disbelief.

'Hmph, hamph, hum.' Una garbled through the tape.

'I think she wants me to untie her.' Aggie said. She soon released the girl's arms and tore away the tape from her

146

mouth. This was a painful operation for poor Una who winced in pain.

'No sense in prolonging the agony!' Aggie explained, recalling her many years of removing plasters from children's cuts and scrapes.

As soon as she was freed Una leapt from the pod and squeezed her rescuer tightly around her very huggable waist.

'Auntie Aggie, you're safe!' She exclaimed through tears of relief. 'I can hardly believe my eyes. I was convinced you must have perished in the sea!'

Not for the first time Aggie was completely mystified having missed the whole drama of her jeep being pushed over the cliff due to her secret visit to the ice cream kiosk. But there was another more urgent issue which stifled any further small talk, for the old handbrake gave a sudden judder and a squeal as the wagon holding the remaining pods began to inch slowly forward and over the cliff edge.

'Gosh, Aggie, we must act quickly. Sebastien and Verity are locked inside those pods too!' Una exclaimed.

The old caretaker acted swiftly. She took up the slack on the chains like a sailor heaving in an anchor and used her body weight to temporarily stabilise the pods while Una, breathless with fright struggled to release the remaining clips.

At last Sebastien and Verity were freed and once relieved of their weight the wagon rested securely on the edge.

Verity stamped her cramped legs furiously and growled like a bear. For the second time in the space of a week she had been bound, gagged and bundled into a claustrophobic little space and she wasn't finding the experience in the least bit amusing.

She took her tablet from a pocket, 'Irate Hostage Vows Revenge on Heartless Captors.' She growled into the microphone through gritted teeth.

Sebastien rubbed the soreness from his wrists and breathed in the fresh salty air, greatly relieved to be out amongst the wide open nature he loved so much and he vowed he would never ever again keep any living creature in captivity.

Then it was time to take stock of the situation.

Firstly, what was to be done about the pods, three with shells cracked open like broken eggs, and beside them the as yet unopened ones containing stolen goods.

There they lay by the cliff edge, waiting for a signal for Ferrit to release the handbrake and send the whole lot tumbling over the edge.

Suddenly Sebastien's face lit with the spark of an idea.

'Why don't we take out the stolen stuff and replace it with bricks and rubble from the alum works? Then we reseal the pods and send them on their journey down the cliff. That way the crooks won't suspect there's anything amiss or that their hostages have escaped!'

'And we'll get to keep the valuable goods for ourselves!' Verity added, eagerly rubbing her hands in glee. She still had a raw urge to inflict revenge on the crooks.

They all agreed this was the best course of action and immediately set to work removing the stolen valuables from each pod before refilling the spaces with loose bricks and mortar.

After a bit of hard work the pods were filled and their clips
locked closed in readiness for a journey down to the sea.
While they waited Sebastien found an abandoned
supermarket trolley which he filled up with the stolen
goods then wheeled into the tall stems of willow.
'It's well hidden and ought to be safe there until we get
home to inform the ......' He was about to say 'police' but
his words were drowned by a violent whiz which rocked
the air followed by a loud explosion. They all froze at the
ear splitting sound.
'The signal!' Una exclaimed at last recovering from the
shock. 'Ferrit was told to wait for a signal to release the
pods. That must be it!'
'Let's do it! Let's set the pods free!' Sebastien and Verity
shouted together in song with a little dance to accompany
the words.
Aggie applied her full strength to the brake handle this time
and the huge metal wheels unlocked.
At first the pods seemed reluctant to leave their station on
the clifftop, the weight of bricks and rubble in their bellies
making movement difficult. So Aggie applied a a hearty
shove and once the first wheel had crept over the edge the
others had no alternative but to follow.
'Bon Voyage and Good Fortune to All Who Sail in Her!'
Verity cried as the wagon and its cargo slipped over the cliff.
The string of pods immediately bounced free from the
wagon to shoot over outcrops of rock, gathering momentum
as they did until eventually all contact with the ground was
lost and the pods were flying through the air like strange
airborne missiles.

As in slow motion, the pods seemed to take an eternity to drop, diminishing smaller and smaller until at last with a huge silent splash, they smacked into the rolling waves far below.

They sank in a sea of froth and for a few heart-stopping moments it seemed they must surely join Davy Jones in his locker deep beneath the sea bed.

But in the next instant one burst through the surface and was followed in quick succession by the others, one by one, until eventually all the pods could be seen bobbing gently up and down on the swell.

'Hey, that was a bit of fun was it not!' Aggie exclaimed, laughing heartily and wiping the rust from her palms.

'It was certainly the highlight of our trip so far.' Una added.

'And finally we have a chapter for the school mag that ends on a high note to balance out all the setbacks of the past weeks.' Verity agreed.

'We certainly have the upper hand over the crooks this time, the thieving magpies.' Sebastien added.

Aggie suddenly remembered something important, something which had been gnawing at the edges of her mind all the while the drama had been unfolding.

'Now come on kids, be honest, where have you hidden my beloved jeep?' She asked.

'Oh dear!' They all exclaimed as one.

Suddenly Aggie's good humoured spirits were about to be dashed on the rocks - rather like her jeep!

Chapter 15

Aggie insisted she must march down the cliff path to inspect the damage at first hand and salvage any belongings that may have survived the fall. Unfortunately she was far from fit and quite unsafe on the steep and slippery path. Una came to the rescue to assist her with a steadying hand at almost every step. It was going to be a long haul!

They had only travelled a few metres when Una suddenly became aware of a sound of fast approaching feet, and the rasp of powerful lungs rapidly closing on her from behind. She had no time to avoid the inevitable collision, and before you could say Jack Robinson four huge paws had bundled her to the floor. She lay out flat with the heavy body panting and pawing around her face and neck.

It was Nelson!

'Nelson! Stop it! Get off me you huge brute!' She yelled.

It took a moment or two but eventually the over zealous dog calmed enough for Una to recover and brush the muddy paw marks from her blouse.

Despite his over exuberant welcome she gave Nelson a hearty hug and squeezed him affectionately.

'It's truly wonderful to see you, Nelson, but you almost knocked me out and then almost licked me to death!' She exclaimed, to which Nelson simply added another lick as if to say, 'Sure, but I can't help it!'

Mr Markham followed behind at a much steadier pace. Una noted he wore the same threadbare clothing as when they last met, and the same scruffy tide mark ringed his neck suggesting he hadn't washed since either.

'What on earth are you doing out here, Mr Markham?' She asked.

'I'm giving Nelson his daily exercise, obviously, But more to the point, what are you doing so far from home?'

Una noted that the elderly gent had his long barrelled gun strapped over a shoulder which she felt was a rather unnecessary accessory for dog walking, but then she guessed old fashioned country gents lived by different standards.

'We're on the case of those villainous crooks.' Verity replied while Una dallied. 'They tried to do away with us by locking us up inside strange insect pods.'

'Actually, we only want to recover anything useful from Auntie Aggie's jeep.' Una corrected her. The thought of tangling with the crooks again sent a cold shiver running down her spine.

'Yes, they intended to catapult us off the cliff to a certain watery death to prevent us squealing to the police so we're going to teach them a lesson or two.' Sebastien added ignoring Una's view that they only wanted to collect bits from the jeep.

'The scoundrels!' Mr Markham exclaimed. 'They need to be locked up, the whole darn lot of them!'

'We'd be happy for you to help us, Mr Markham.' Sebastien suggested hopefully. It was evident to Una that her friends were more focused on revenge than on recovering Aggie's possessions.

'I for one would feel a whole lot safer with Nelson on our side.' She said resigning herself to the fate of an inevitable clash with the crooks.

Mr Markham was all enthusiasm and needed little persuasion.

'Too right I'll join you.' He said. 'I've a grudge or two myself to square up with that wormy lot. They broke into my home and would have killed me had it not been for you kids and Nelson. Yes, I'd love to even up the score with the dastardly rogues!'

'Me too! You should see the mess they've made of my beautiful jeep!' Aggie added eager to join rank with the old gent.

Down they filed, Mr Markham proving a useful companion for Aggie linking arms to guide her safely over the steps, although it did occur to Una that if Aggie happened to slip he would almost certainly be dragged down with her!

While she went down and down ever closer to the sea, Una began to think about Edward again. He had not put in an appearance since the crooks had captured her. She was still cross with him. This habit he had of disappearing whenever he was needed infuriated her.

That last time when Tinker had locked her in the pod he had simply vanished from the rocks and left Aggie to do all the rescuing.

No doubt he would make up one of his lame excuses about the unpredictable nature of time travel. Una was beginning to suspect that Edward used time travel as an excuse, a weak apology to avoid taking responsibility for his own lack of action.

She made a mental note to confront him about the issue next time he put in an appearance. She must pin him down and get to the bottom of the problem.

Stopping to catch her breath Una caught a glimpse of the sea rippling like foil far below and beyond that the tiny hamlet of Robin Hood's Bay with its street lamps blinking like fairy lights against the approaching gloom of evening. She pushed thoughts of Edward from her mind so as to concentrate on the ever steeper and uneven scramble down the path.

As they closed on the beach Una began to worry about the incoming tide. On her previous visit the flooding waves had forced her to make an emergency exit, a scramble up the cliff to avoid being drowned. After that frightening experience she had vowed never again to put herself in such dire peril.

At last, after what seemed an eternity of climbing the group arrived to a narrow shelf of grass, set back from the edge, where they might rest in the shadows, hidden from sight. Aggie lay flat on her back gulping in air for all the world like a stranded whale. Mr Markham opened a flask of water and quenched Nelson's thirst. Sebastien had his attention taken by an early evening barn owl hunting along the ledges and hollows of the cliff. The sharp eyed predator ghosted silently up and down looking for a late meal.

A short distance away the half submerged remains of Aggie's jeep swayed in rhythm to the swell, salt water dancing in and out of the smashed windscreen.

Over to the right Una checked out the crooks as they worked to recover the string of pods. Tugging on the chains and hugging the wet, slippery edges they lifted the awkward shells one at a time onto the deck of the swaying boat.

'Looks like they're tidying up and getting ready to heave anchor.' Mr Markham observed. He contemplated the scene a while in silence as the crooks collected a few remaining pieces of equipment from the shoreline.

'I've a mind to hot foot it down there and give them all a good hiding!' Aggie threatened, as she noticed for the first time the mangled wreckage of her beloved jeep.

Mr Markham agreed with her. 'We have a duty as law abiding citizens to stop those rotten thieves in their tracks by whatever means we have.'

'In that case, we need to take action right away or they're going to escape!' Sebastien said.

Mr Markham furrowed his brows in concentration then declared.

'Right kids and madam, gather around and listen in to my plan of action!'

He began to amass a little heap of items on the grass bank. The collection included a rock, a pile of pebbles, several seashells of various shapes and sizes, some oddments of wood and a tangle of bright orange fisherman's netting.

'Pretty art arrangement, Mr Markham, but what about the plan to stop the crooks?' Verity asked.

'Be patient, child! All of these objects represent various key elements in the plan which we will use to overcome the crooks!' He deliberately placed a fragment of wood at the centre.

'This piece of wood is the boat, the pebbles represent each of the crooks and we are the shells.' He placed the pebbles on top of the wood and scattered the shells to various directions.

155

Then Mr Markham outlined his master plan, moving and arranging the items like a game of chess. He was like a Napoleon organising the movement of his troops in one of those brilliant military campaigns.

The pebbles shifted this way, the shells made a pincer movement in that and the wooden fragment bobbed about on the grass in the middle. A little drama played out before the audience before concluding with the pebbles being surrounded by the shells and surrendering.

It all seemed too easy to Una, but Mr Markham assured her everything would pan out just as he planned providing everyone played their part. So all being briefed the troops took up their positions and prepared for action.

Aggie and Una set off the campaign, frantically waving their arms from a small island where they had taken up position.

'Help! Someone please help us! We're stranded on this tiny island.'

'We need help or we'll be washed into the sea and drowned!'

Their cries were to no avail however, the crooks being far to engrossed in their work to notice their pleas and the pair had nothing more to show for their efforts other than sore throats.

In the end Aggie resolved the situation by hoisting a large boulder to her shoulder and propelling it across the waves like an Olympic shot-put thrower. The missile crashed into the sea just metres from the boat.

Now they had the full attention of the crooks who believed they were under attack from cannon fire.

'It's that pesky girl and the old woman! How on earth did they escape alive?' Tinker shrieked when he saw the pair waving.

'You three nip ashore and capture them. Rough them up a bit if you need to, then later we'll feed them to the fishes. People'll think they've been caught out by the incoming tide and drowned.'

Richter plus the two heavies armed themselves with wooden batons, splashed into the shallows and headed menacingly towards Aggie and Una.

As planned, These two quickly retreated back up the path and took up new positions on a ledge where Verity awaited armed with a stash of large stones.

Their brief from Mr Markham was simple: 'If they attack, use your height advantage to rain down showers of stones on them....' Adding the worse case scenario instruction... 'if that fails, run for it!'

Aggie didn't hold out much hope of being able to outrun any of the physically fit crooks, but she did on the other hand feel more than a match for any one of them in a hand to hand duel, especially given her long experience of dealing with problem children and stroppy teachers. More than that, she secretly harboured a malicious desire to rough up one or two of them in retribution for what they'd done to her precious jeep and she was all keyed up for a confrontation.

While this little game of cat and mouse played out Mr Markham and Sebastien had slithered down the blind side of the beach ready to board the boat unseen, making good use of the smoke-screen created by Aggie and Una. Now

they had lured away most of the crooks the prize of
capturing the boat fell well within their means.

But it was not to be all plain sailing. A tall pinnacle of rock,
like a wall jutted across their path, perfect for cover but
razor sharp to the touch.

Mr Markham ordered Sebastien to remove his shoes and
socks, replacing the shoes on his feet and pulling the socks
over his hands. Mr Markham did likewise and now they
were able to close in on the swaying boat without slashing
their hands to ribbons.

As they approached Tinker was preoccupied hauling in the
last of the pods completely unaware that he was about to be
joined by a pair of uninvited guests.

The old gentleman stood outlined black against the dull red
of the darkening sky, like a pensioner version of Indiana
Jones. He tensed his muscles taut, heavy boots gripping
rock. For a second the slippery deck hovered within
millimetres of his toes, but the sea swelled up and down
randomly making the leap unpredictable and hazardous.
Then suddenly taking his chance Mr Markham leapt across
the void.

He landed with a thud on the poop deck and the sudden
impact caused the whole boat to dip wildly downwards on
one side and then just as quickly buck back upwards like a
rodeo bull.

The unfortunate Tinker was catapulted over the side
landing with an almighty splash face down in the salty
brine.

Sebastien now leapt nimble footed to join Mr Markham on the deck just in time to see Tinker's mouth surface and gulp in a breath of air.

Tinker swam the short distance to the beach, but on seeing Nelson there pawing the sand and growling on the strand line the crook thought twice about getting out of the water and instead about turned to the boat.

But this strategy failed too as Mr Markham was waiting for him on the deck, and each time Tinker tried to climb onto the boat the old gent gave him a sharp prod with the pointed end of his gun.

Eventually, cold and tired Tinker gave up and swam back to the beach in the hope that Nelson's growl was worse than his bite and there he lay exhausted on the sand.

Having successfully secured the boat Sebastien and Mr Markham turned their attentions to the cliff to assess how the other half of their team was faring. It was not a happy scene.

Una, Aggie and Verity had run out of pebbles and now three bruised and irate crooks were on the point of capturing them. Richter arrived first and quickly subdued Verity while the two heavies clamped their arms on Aggie intending to bring her to the ground.

But the old caretaker had no intention of coming quietly. She threw back an arm the size of a leg of mutton and landed a massive punch on the chin of the nearest. He dropped like a bag of flour. The second drew back nervously reluctant to risk suffering the same fate.

But Richter, who by now had subdued Verity rushed to assist his stricken colleagues and after a brief struggle Aggie was finally overpowered by sheer weight of numbers. Sebastien, watching from the boat saw Una hesitate, torn between loyalty to her friends and the need to escape.

'Run for it, Una!' Sebastien yelled. Una stiffened and appeared to prepare herself for flight, but instead chose to stand by her friends, was overwhelmed by the much stronger crooks and quickly surrendered.

Three crooks frogmarched the prisoners down to the little stretch of beach where they were joined by Tinker who had recovered from his swim, but still looked thoroughly miserable. He wrung out his dripping shirt and poured water from his shoes. He brushed the salt from his eye patch and set it back in place over his eye.

That done Tinker quickly regained his composure almost as if the patch had magical properties which infused the wearer with instant sprinkles of confidence. He ordered Una, Verity and Aunt Aggie to be lined up on the shoreline then hollered across to Mr Markham and Sebastien.

'Bring the boat to the shore and give yourselves up. We have your friends here and they may get horribly injured if you refuse to be sensible.' As if to prove his point he lifted Una by her long black hair until only her toes teetered and danced with the ground.

'No way! We have your boat with its precious cargo of stolen property.' Mr Markham shouted back, patting the row of pods arranged on the deck. 'If you so much as lay a finger on our friends we'll dump this whole caboodle over the side and all your dirty thieving will be for nothing.' He was in no mood to do business with the crooks and like Tinker was unaware that the pods had been filled with worthless rubble and the loot hidden on top of the cliff. Tinker's face reddened with rage. He gathered his cronies in a scrum for a parley.

After some heated debate they came up with a plan and Tinker returned to make a compromise using his most humblest of negotiation tones.

'Look kids, we don't want any trouble. All we want is our honestly acquired stolen property that rightfully belongs to us. Surely we can be sensible about this situation we find ourselves in and come to an amiable compromise?'

'Such as what?' Mr Markham barked back.

'Supposing we let your friends go free? You'd like that wouldn't you? We'll allow them to start climbing up the cliff path and once you're happy they're safe, you draw the boat to the shore. You and the boy jump out on one side while we climb in from the other.'

'It's a win, win situation for all and everyone goes home happy.' Richter added with his best hyena smile.

'Let's do it!' Sebastien said, thinking only of the safety of his friends on the shore. 'I think it's a good deal.'

'A good deal my foot!' Mr Markham spat out.' I wouldn't trust that crook as far as you can throw a deaf rabbit.'

Sebastien's mind wrestled with the image of someone throwing a deaf rabbit as the boat rocked beneath his feet.

Mr Markham leered at the crooks on the beach and they smiled back expectantly. Una and the other hostages simply looked cold and miserable waiting on the shore, pondering their fate. It seemed to Sebastien the tense stand-off could never be broken.

But broken it was, and in the most unexpected of circumstances.

The door to the boat's tiny cabin was suddenly thrown open and to everyone's astonishment Amphety came barging out, a pistol pointed directly to Mr Markham's head.

This sudden intrusion took everyone unawares. But the shock of the woman appearing so unexpectedly was nothing compared to the utter shock and horror of the terrible transformation which her facial features had undergone in the space of a few short days.

For the immaculate, unblemished skin and dark facial features which had so cast a spell and hypnotised anyone who had gazed upon her beauty was now gone.

Incredibly, her skin had turned a deathly pale and her rosy cheeks turned wrinkled, faded and with the texture of old blotting paper. Her blue eyes, once remarkable for their enchanting twinkle were now a dull grey, set in dark hollows, and shot with veins of ruby blood.

In fact, she had become so very ill of recent days that she had slept soundly through the whole drama which had unfolded on the deck.

'Move the boat to the shore!' She ordered Mr Markham in a cracked whisper. She waved the pistol in a threatening arc and drew a pale finger to the trigger.

Mr Markham turned his own much bigger weapon to bear on the woman and lined up the barrels to point directly between her bloodshot eyes.

'Not on your life, missus! Drop your weapon or I'll blow your brains to shredded wheat!' He said gravely.

The woman threw her head back and gave a cruel laugh which revealed a set of algae stained teeth and green pus filled gums, sure signs of severe poisoning.

'Go ahead, shoot me. That old rust bucket hasn't been fired in anger since Oliver Cromwell's days. You're more likely to blow your own brains out than mine!'

'Well, don't say I didn't warn you!' Mr Markham replied sternly and his finger squeezed the trigger.

The hammer struck down with a sharp click, but instead of thunder and explosion, it gave a pathetic fizz and was followed by a thin puff of smoke which trailed away into the night air like candy-floss.

Old Mr Markham looked down the barrel in despair.

'Darn, that's torn it!' He exclaimed and dropped the weapon to the deck to raise his hands in surrender.

Chapter 16

'Tonight we fish with live bait.' Tinker announced as he hoisted the anchor to rest by the boat's rail. A loop of rope trailed across the deck with a tight knot around each prisoner's ankle. It started from the anchor at one end and concluded in a double knot around Mr Markham's boney shin at the other.

'The sharks will make short work of these lovely juicy bodies and the crabs will snip away at their bones. By morning no trace of our guests will remain except perhaps for a handful of loose teeth which the mermaids will use to make fine ivory necklaces for adorning their beautiful necks!'

The heavies seated in the stern laughed heartily at Tinker's good natured humour and gave a round of applause. Evening had arrived quite suddenly and a splattering of stars broke through the night sky, the type of stars you only see from the deck of a boat in the wide ocean when all around you is pitch blackness.

The quiet was broken every now and again by a thud and a judder as a wave struck the bow and the prisoners were clattered from side to side like ten pin bowls.

'Don't worry about the stormy crossing, in a few minutes you'll all be taking a swim fathoms down to Davey Jones' locker.' Tinker patted one of the insect pods fondly as if stroking a loyal pet.

'As you sink you might like to think of us, speeding across the sea to freedom with our pods full of unimaginable riches. Wealth enough for us to live like royalty for the rest of our lives!'

'Well, you'll be getting the biggest shock of your lives because the pods are all empty! We've taken out your precious stolen property and replaced it with worthless junk! There's nothing inside them but bricks and rubble, so instead of luxury you'll be spending the rest of your lives in poverty.' Una replied.

'And every day you'll wish you'd been kinder to us kids!' Verity added.

Tinker smirked. 'You don't think I'd fall for that old herring, do you? I can tell by the sound when they're struck that these lovely pods are stuffed full with treasure.'

'No, they're full of rocks, and don't think we'll tell you where we've hidden the stolen stuff because we'll never squeak.' Sebastien said in a whisper. He knew they were in dire straits, even if Tinker did discover the true contents of the pods their situation could hardly be worse.

They were in deep water, rather like the boat itself which was being tossed about like a rag in a washing machine. Amphety came down the line to ensure the knots were all secure, stopping to shine a torch into each prisoner's face as she passed along.

When at length she came to Una she halted frozen as a statue, the torch beam burning directly into her eyes. Una squinted back into the withered yellow face with its dark, hollow eye sockets.

'I remember you!' She suddenly croaked. 'You're the girl from the bookshop!' You could see her mind searching back through her memories, slowly piecing together details of a half forgotten incident. Then she suddenly recalled lucidly how on that day she had so wanted to break the girl's wrists, to inflict pain on her, so infuriating was her expression of childish innocence.

When the penny dropped Amphety began to fish about in her pockets searching for the forgotten object. Her withered fingers stretched into the deepest recesses and emerged clutching a small metal toy.

'This is it!' She cried. 'This is it, the curse and cause of all my illnesses.' She held the toy soldier aloft for all to see, the same toy she'd stolen from Una's satchel.

'You've used it to poison me, to cast a spell of illness over me!' She said in accusing tones.

'You stole it from me!' Una shot back. 'Never expect good to come from an act of evil!'

'Well, I'll have no more of it.' Amphety replied, her shrill voice rising to a pitch, and she tossed the precious little toy into the black waters. It hit like a stone with a dull splash and sank in less than a moment. She returned to the stern where Tinker was securing the pods ready for poor weather.

'Is the water deep enough to dump the prisoners now?' She asked. Tinker tested the depth using a boat hook.

'I do believe it is. Let's have the dirty deed done and get some shut-eye before morning.'

Lifting together the two heavies hoisted the anchor to the starboard rail ready to drop over the side, but as they called out a first 'heave ho!' the boat juddered under a sudden force.

Both men lost their footing and tumbled in a heap onto the deck. The anchor came crashing down between their splayed feet.

'What on earth was that, a freak wave or something?' Tinker asked.

No sooner had the first judder subsided than a second one ripped through the hull throwing everyone who had stood back to the deck floor.

Then a third jolt followed as regular as clockwork.

Each jolt slowed the boat's progress until eventually the boat actually began to travel in a backwards direction.

Waves spilled over the stern and water flooded over the wooden decking. It seemed the boat was headed back to the beach from whence it had originally set out.

'What in Poseidon's name is going on?' Tinker asked incredulously.

Richter peered over the stern. 'As far as I can tell boss, the boat has got snagged on a rope or something of the sort and it's being dragged backwards.'

'Then engage the engines full ahead!' Tinker ordered.

The heavy at the wheel obeyed and a screech of powerful engines filled the air accompanied by dense clouds of oily black smoke. Saltwater boiled up in eddies at the stern and the boat dipped dangerously low as a huge wave of water arose out of the sea and swamped the poop deck.

'It's no good, the propeller must be caught up in a tangle of old fishing line or something.' Richter shouted from the stern.

It was a guess, for the night was far too black to see through the murky waters, all he knew for sure was the boat was being dragged backwards, back to land rather than out across the sea to freedom.

'Then give her all you've got and a bit of extra for good measure.' Tinker ordered.

Once again the heavy behind the wheel revved the engines and the propeller churned out water like a demonic food mixer.

In a moment the air filled with the dangerous smell of overheating metal. A flash of flame, electric sparks and a loud explosion ripped through the wooden deck-boards and the boat filled with flames and a dense cloud of choking black smoke. The second heavy rushed in with a fire extinguisher and doused the flames.

All went strangely silent, except for the gentle, rhythmical lap of water butting against the hull. It seemed the drama was over and nothing more than a tiresome row back to shore was to follow.

Not so, another jolt shook the hull, so violently this time that it caused everyone standing to keel over yet again.

Now the boat pulled freely back towards the shore like a magnet attracted to its opposite pole, only this time without the engines striving in an opposing direction. The boat quickly picked up momentum, moving with a pulse of regular jerks towards the beach.

The crooks were far too pre-occupied with the strange turn of events to complete the task of throwing the anchor overboard. Instead they waited in a stunned awe wondering what on earth was to follow next.

'Could it be a pod of whales clinging to the keel?' Richter wondered.

'Balderdash!' Tinker exclaimed. 'Someone's pulling us hand over hand back to the beach!'

It was a preposterous suggestion, one still more unlikely than a pod of whales, and yet the regular pulse did indeed give the impression of a deliberate force hauling the boat in reverse.

'We should drop anchor.' Amphety yelled. 'Let's gift the whales a present with bodies attached and see how they like that!' Using every ounce of her strength she lifted the anchor over the top rail and despatched the huge block overboard. It disappeared with a dull sploosh into the sea. The coil of rope followed as it must, like a frantic snake jumping and jerking over the rails. Una braced herself in the sure knowledge that she too must follow, dragged with it by the knot of rope.

But no, the rope suddenly sagged and drooped loosely, and so the dreadful wrench didn't come. Instead Una was able to peer over the bow into the water in time to see the anchor floating away on the surface as if it had only the weight of a helium balloon.

And then that most unlikeliest of possibilities which Tinker had suggested was confirmed to be true when out of the waves there emerged twenty men, ten pairs on either side of the bow, each pair heaving on taught ropes attached to the underside of the boat.

They must have been unusually tall men, Una thought, to walk tiptoe on the seabed and yet still stand head and shoulder above the waves. She realised they must be no ordinary men, not even humans to survive without air so long underwater.

Their grey hair dripped, their eyes stared directly ahead and their grey faces set firm in concentration. They seemed unaware of anything beyond their core task of hauling the boat to shore.

Now two more grey men emerged carrying the anchor across their shoulders to take up their rank alongside the boat's hull.

Finally from the murky waters there came striding a monstrous creature unlike anything Una had ever witnessed before in her life.

It was a bizarre octopus-like giant of near two metres in height, covered entirely in slithery knots of seaweed; long leathery belts of oarweed, bangles of olive bladderwrack, clattering purple mussel shells, green sea lettuce, razor shells and mermaid's purses. The whole tangled mass glistening and dripping as the creature laboured itself from the waves.

This truly macabre vision caused all those gathered on the deck to quail and quake in fear for their safety. Yet despite the creature's frightful presence their attention was nonetheless drawn away by some shadowy movements on the little strip of sand between sea and cliff.

Gigantic crabs crawling from the sea, was Una's first thought, but on closer inspection she realised the shapes were in fact men and women, some fifty or so, slowly descending the cliff path and gathering quietly in an arc along the beach.

At their head, and remarkable for their heights and fair complexions, came a handsome young man and an enchanting woman each of a similar age. Una searched her mind for a word to describe the pair and in the end settled on 'noble,' despite their simple working attire.

The giant octopus creature shuffled forward awkwardly on the land until it settled directly between the noble pair dwarfing even those two stately individuals.

Now the boat had been drawn up to the beach and the grey men let go the ropes and deposited the anchor on the shoreline. They freed the captives from their shackles allowing each to disembark safely and lowering the children carefully to the sand in their safe arms.

The thieves were less keen to leave the safety of the boat and be set loose among the noisy grey crowd who they suspected may have hostile intentions.

When several of the grey men, hair dripping with seaweed and beards foaming with spray climbed aboard the boat to assist them down Tinker raised his gun in defiance.

'You are trespassers. Remove yourselves from my boat forthwith or I will have no option but to shoot in self defence.' He warned.

By way of response, the first grey giant took Richter by his neck and knees and hoisted the screaming man over the rail where he was ably caught in mid-air by a second and set down heavily on the beach where he remained huddled in a heap shivering with fright.

The next grey man then closed in on Tinker intending to escort him down likewise.

'Don't say I didn't warn you!' Tinker cried and he fired off a shot directly between the man's eyes from point blank range. Then, for good measure he fired off two more shots at the grey man's companions.

Tinker couldn't fail but score direct hits from such close quarters and the trio of bullets cracked like thunder in the night. But the salvo passed directly through the grey men's heads leaving behind a thin trail of dust.

The shot men halted abruptly, in shock or surprise. Perhaps they had never before witnessed the awesome power of such a potent weapon, although as alum workers they were certainly familiar enough with ear splitting explosions. However, as the dust settled it became apparent the men were completely unharmed. The bullets had passed directly through their heads! This apparent proof of invincibility brought to a swift end any further resistance from Tinker and his crew. One by one they were dropped from the deck by the grey men and handed down to the beach.

The crowd that had gathered on the rocks and shoreline now struck up candlelights until the narrow ledges along the cliffs where they assembled were bathed in orbs of flickering yellow light.

The scene reminded Una of a spectacular outdoor theatre; the arc of audience filling the stalls eagerly awaiting the show to begin, the main performers of giant octopus and noble twins holding centre stage and the minor cast members of crooks and children assembled in the wings to stage left and right.

Yet this gathering of ghostly villagers had not descended the steep cliffs in the darkness to be entertained. No, in fact they had been summoned there by the village elders to attend a court of sorts, and it soon became apparent that it was the crooks who were to face trial.

A bell rang to signal an opening of proceedings and a hush descended across the little beach. The giant octopus or whatever it was tripped forward ready to address the audience, and so the trial began.

'Greetings villagers of Ravenscar, the ghosts of workers in many trades, ordinary people, you who have scratched a living from the precious alum on this bleak coastline for over a hundred years.' The octopus began in strange gruff tones, difficult on the ears which caused all there to strain intently to catch the words.

At his words each person in the audience turned to examine their neighbour as if seeing them there for the first time. They saw hard men clad in leather aprons, warm woollen jackets and tough leather footwear. They saw the weather worn faces of women in domestic attire and their children and babies, dirty faced and with the grime of labour on their hands.

'Into your honest working community, so many years untainted by crime, has come a dark stain in the form of the rabble of crooks you see brought before you today. These evil crooks, in pursuit of their own greedy wants and desires have intended to bring harm on the innocent children who the working men of your village have rescued today.'

The octopus pointed a bunch of leathery arm at the crooks and then in turn across to the children. The villagers turned to stare first at the shamefaced crooks and then across to the bewildered children. Una was reminded for a moment of the spectators at a tennis match.

'Had it not been for these brave alum workers, summoned today from their peaceful places of rest, not only gross theft, but also foul murder would certainly have been committed on these dark cliffs.'

The crowd gasped in horror.

'They wrecked my jeep too!' Aggie blurted out, not wishing the destruction of her precious vehicle to be omitted from the catalogue of crimes.

The monster waved an octet of withered arms and the hollow chambers of seaweed rattled like snare drums. The royal twins, for it seemed certain the noble pair were such, pressed closer to the monster almost as they might to a dear friend.

A whispered conversation took place between the three after which the octopus withdrew and the man and woman stepped graciously forward to take the centre stage. Once again the audience hushed in anticipation.

'We are not a criminal court here to convict you of your crimes and beyond the boundaries of these ancient alum works we have no authority to do so.' The woman began in a kindly yet commanding voice.

'That is indeed so.' The noble man continued. 'My sister and I are merely the elected protectors of this ancient community. We are pledged with a duty of care for the good and safety of the cliffs and for the people who have made this place their home over many centuries.'

'We are indeed the caring guardians responsible for the people you see gathered here before you today and for all who have followed since.'

'We intend to offer you two choices.' The man continued while the bedraggled crooks shivered with cold in the wings as they awaited their fate.

'The choices each have consequences so you must decide wisely.' The woman warned.

'I'm not going to be told what to do, it's not in my nature.' Tinker declared and he made as to leave, but before he had taken four strides a pair of grey guards clamped their hands firmly around his arms and frogmarched him unceremoniously back to his allocated place between Richter, Amphety and the two heavies.

'Have grace and listen to the options we are to grant you!' The man ordered sternly. There was a momentary pause while Tinker examined the bruises to his arms and complained about injustice and the lack of human rights and the like, then the woman continued.

'You may freely depart from this place and our ancient community, but if you choose to do so you must vow never again to return to tarnish our coastline and cliffs.' She declared.

'And if we refuse, what then?' Tinker demanded.

'The alternative for you, if you so choose is to remain here, to continue your evil plans and your criminal activities.' The man replied and his words brought a smile of approval from Tinker.

'But if you choose to do so, these people, the ghosts of the alum workers, the grey men and their families, will haunt you for the rest of your lives…and beyond.' The woman warned sternly and promptly wiped the grin from Tinker's face.

Tinker, Amphety, Richter and the two heavies, who had been so unkind and so ruthless towards the children until now, were reduced to shivering wrecks and cowered in fear for their lives surrounded as they were by the unnatural grey men. Not to mention the giant octopus which still hovered menacingly close by.

They had no desire other than to flee from the dreadful cliffs with their lives intact and to escape the living nightmare of the grey men.

'Please, allow us to go and we promise never to return.' Richter cried.

'I swear we'll never set foot on these bleak hills ever again.' The two heavies declared.

'For sure, I never want to set eyes on this place or its people again, not in this lifetime nor the next.' Tinker agreed and he rubbed his aching arms and glared at the grey giants who had restrained him.

'In that case you should leave without delay, for many of the grey men gathered in this place would be pleased to crush your bones to a powder and feed it to the fishes, much as you had intended for your victims.' The noble woman pointed her slender arm towards the cliff path.

Tinker and his crew led away dismally up the cliff, and despite the darkness made good haste, like goats returning for their evening meal, and it was not long before their fleeing shapes had melted away into the night.

Once they were truly gone the giant octopus thanked the alum workers and the grey men and their families for their support and one by one they dispersed like mist into the darkness, almost as if they had never really existed.

The brother and sister directed a low bow and broad smiles at the giant octopus causing Una to wonder at what strange relationship existed between them. The octopus returned the greeting with a rattle of numerous arms and legs then returned their bows with a noisy clanking of his own joints. The noble twins waved a fond farewell as they climbed the steep path until they too were lost to sight.

Now only Aggie, Mr Markham and Nelson and the three children remained on the thin strip of beach with the giant octopus creature a slight distance apart.

And then something quite strange occurred which only Una saw in its full entirety. The giant octopus turned away and tottered unsteadily towards the water's edge intending no doubt to return to its rightful home in the deep.

But in the gloom one misplaced tentacle tripped on a particularly long strand of slippery seaweed. The creature skidded and the whole mass of seaweed and shells and all the other nautical adornments were suddenly dragged from its body almost as if it had been skinned alive. They were left in a pile, a pyramid of glistening seaweed on the shoreline.

For those on the beach, a kind of magic occurred, for it seemed to them that the sea monster had simply dissolved into nothingness. No trace of the beast remained other than the mass of weed heaped at the water's edge.

But for Una a different kind of magic occurred, for at the same moment as the seaweed slipped to the ground, she observed a pair of hands emerge from underneath. The hands lifted the mass of seaweed into the air then dropped it on the shore to reveal Edward hiding inside, invisible to all but Una.

Edward emerged grinning from ear to ear! Una was astonished.

'Good evening, Una.' He said in his gruff pretend monster voice.

'Edward! I might have known it was you!' She exclaimed and dashed over to greet him, throwing her arms around his neck and hugging him tightly. Edward smiled with pleasure in the knowledge he had so thoroughly tricked her.

'Come, follow me a little way, I must tell you of my adventures.' He said and the group on the beach watched Una skip away alone.

Edward led between the rocky outcrops with the sound of the sea always to the left and the black cliff face rising to the right.

'I'm sure you'd like me to update you on my daring plan to rescue the boy and girl?' He said after a while.

'Tell me, but I've already guessed it!' Una replied.

'You have?'

'I feel sure they must be the two guardians who spoke on behalf of the workers tonight.' Una guessed.

'You're right, Una!' Edward confirmed. 'Through luck by my own determination, and the assistance of a young man with a cap, I was able to rescue them both from a runaway railway wagon which would otherwise have resulted in disaster.'

'So rather than perish the children grew to have full lives and became much valued members of the alum community?' Una guessed again.

Edward was impressed by her insight.

'Yes, indeed. So you saw with your own eyes how important to their community the two children had become! They are proof that my interference with the course of time has brought about positive change not just for the two children but for the alum people too.' Edward stated proud of his achievement.

They came now to the tiny cove where on a previous visit Edward had pointed out the stone marker, but now nothing remained there, no carved hollow, no stone post. The tragedy had not occurred.

'One thing I don't understand is how you are now able to touch and be seen by those people of alum?' Una wanted to know.

'That's a good question, Una. I think the more I slip through time the greater the control I have over my being. Like I'm discovering mind over matter.' Edward said, but it was difficult for him to explain something which he didn't fully understand himself.

'I have a gift from the deep for you.' He said to avoid any more difficult questions and he handed Una a small parcel loosely wrapped in seaweed.

She felt the weight and immediately know what it must be. She carefully prised apart the leathery strands and found the little lead soldier neatly wrapped inside.

'You rescued it for me!' She exclaimed. But when she looked up Edward's bright cheeks and twinkling eyes were no longer there. She was alone on the beach.

The boat had broken from its mooring and was bobbing away into the distance, a Marie Celeste if ever there was one.

They were all too tired from the adventures of the day to climb the steep path, and in any case it was dangerous in the darkness. So instead they found a sheltered spot between a group of rocks set above the beach and rested there an hour til daylight came.

The new day brought a welcome touch of warmth and a glow of red streaks to the pale horizon. Aggie who always rose early anyway, lifted her skirt and paddled out to salvage odd bits from her jeep while the others stretched to loosen their stiff muscles.

'I guess it's the bus home for us.' Aggie declared once she'd returned, her arms full of belongings and her skirt dripping with salt water. 'Follow me, folks!' And she set out up the steep ascent.

The End

Printed in Great Britain
by Amazon

76911075R00108